Cherish Me, Cowboy

Cherish Me, Cowboy

A Wildflower Ranch Novella

Alissa Callen

TULE
PUBLISHING

Cherish Me, Cowboy
Copyright © 2014 Alissa Callen
Tule Publishing First Printing, May 2018

The Tule Publishing Group, LLC

ALL RIGHTS RESERVED

No part of this book may be used or reproduced in any manner whatsoever without written permission except in the case of brief quotations embodied in critical articles and reviews.

This is a work of fiction. Names, characters, places, and incidents are products of the author's imagination or are used fictitiously. Any resemblance to actual events, locales, organizations, or persons, living or dead, is entirely coincidental

ISBN: 978-1-949068-30-6

Dedication

*To fabulous Jane Porter and the marvelous
Tule Publishing team.
Pure magic happens in Marietta, Montana.*

Chapter One

THE NEXT TIME Payton Hollis went to a wedding she'd wear boots.

Her work-roughened fingers fumbled with the delicate clasp of her sky-high sandal. "Dammit."

It would be Christmas before her foot slipped free from its candy-pink prison. She chewed the last of the gloss from her bottom lip and glanced at the prone body of the newborn calf on the other side of the wire fence.

"Hang in there, buddy. I'm coming."

She pulled hard at the diamante buckle winking in the late afternoon sunlight and the clasp finally surrendered. Her sigh of relief blew the strands of brown hair out of her eyes. The next wedding she went to she'd also wear her hat.

Payton tossed the sandal to join its partner on the battered passenger seat of her pickup and rummaged around for her old boots. Her favorite pair had split above their worn heels and she'd stored them in her truck for when she found the money to fix them. They'd been there a while.

She pulled on the soft leather and her feet sighed. Mandy

Wright could remind her a thousand times what a bargain the strappy pink sandals were but next trip to Marietta she'd donate them to the thrift store they'd found them in.

The dry autumn wind tugged at her loose hair as she slid into the driver's seat. Through the dusty windshield, the rugged Absaroka mountain range pushed out of the rolling green foothills of Paradise Valley. She only had to look a little to her left to see where the green faded into a parched brown. Her great-grandfather may have named their ranch after the local white conical wildflower but no flowers, let alone grass, swayed in the breeze. Beargrass Hills Ranch had missed all the spring storms as well as the summer squalls. The prairie was bare, the cattle hungry and her water supply critical.

She turned the ignition key. She'd swing out across the road, back up to the fence and lower the tailgate so she could jump from the platform over the fence. The truck engine idled as she waited for a silver car to pass.

Out her side window, Payton checked on the black Angus cow suckling a tiny calf. When she'd left for Eliza's wedding she'd known the cow would calve that afternoon but if she'd known she'd deliver twins, she'd never have left her alone. At least the twins had arrived safely and one of the newborn calves was doing okay. It wasn't uncommon for the second calf to be rejected and Payton had a few tricks up her cowgirl sleeve to ensure the calf would survive. But before she could do anything she had to get the calf to the barn and make sure the little critter had a feed of antibody-rich milk.

Her thumbs tapped on the steering wheel as the silver car drew closer. "Move along," she muttered as the glossy sedan slowed, "there's nothing to see here."

Her stomach grumbled as she breathed in the rich aroma of the plate of foil-covered prime ribs safe on the floor of the truck. Her early lunch was little more than a vague memory. When she'd told Eliza she was worried about the cow and couldn't stay for the reception held at The Graff Hotel, her kind-hearted friend had organized a plate of food for her to take home. She smiled. Seth was one lucky cowboy and Eliza was one happy cowgirl.

Payton's smile died as she stifled an unexpected pang of loneliness. Where had that come from? The joy shining in Eliza's eyes as she'd said her wedding vows must have affected her more than she thought. She had no time, or room, in her life for a man let alone to feel lonely. She had her friends, ranch and cows. That was all she needed, wasn't it?

The male driver pulled off the road and parked the silver sedan on the verge. She released a tight breath of frustration. Now was not the time for some bored wedding guest to make a stop on their scenic Montana tour while the bride and groom had their photographs taken. She had a calf to feed and then re-mother.

Payton switched off the engine. She'd fielded her share of curious questions when her father had turned Beargrass Hills into a dude ranch during her teens. She rolled down her window. She'd dig deep into her well of zen calm and send the out-of-towner on their way.

A broad-shouldered and lean-hipped figure uncurled himself from the driver's side seat. She briefly closed her eyes. City-slicker. Then she took another look. This man might wear fancy shoes and a tailored suit but there was nothing soft about the hard line of his jaw or the swagger in his stride.

"Everything okay?" he asked, his deep voice low and slow as he reached the truck's open window. He pushed his designer sunglasses onto the top of his short, dark hair.

Payton stared into blue eyes as clear as a spring-fed summer lake. For an endless second the world fell away before the breeze carried the scent of high-end aftershave and reminded her she already had more than enough blue-eyed masculine trouble.

"Fine, thanks."

From long practice, she held his gaze. First impressions were created in ten seconds. This wedding guest needed to see past her fine bones and small size to her strength and capability. She'd fought hard against the genetic card she'd been dealt. Mandy might envy her petite figure but she refused to be treated as though she were spun from fragile glass. She was as tough and as able as any man.

The stranger's eyes narrowed. She didn't look away.

"So you don't want any help with that lone calf over

there."

She blinked. Since when did a businessman notice abandoned calves.

"Nope."

"Are you sure?" She didn't know if it was the slight drawl to his tone or the quirk of the corner of his mouth that caused her breath to catch. "Because I'm sure pink cocktail dresses aren't in a cowgirl's manual of what to wear when jumping over a barbed wire fence."

Despite herself, she smiled. Funny as well as gorgeous. Mandy had sure missed this guest at the church when she'd bemoaned the lack of fresh eye-candy.

She clipped on her seat belt and glanced at the strapless and flimsy dress that was as impractical as a show pony in a barrel-race.

"So would that be the sassy and modern cowgirls' manual? Because on page three it clearly says anything pink goes. Now if you don't mind, I have a calf to rescue."

The man dipped his head and grinned. "Be my guest."

Her gaze lingered. She had the strange impression he'd look right at home doffing a cowboy hat.

"Enjoy your visit to Montana and ... thanks for checking everything was okay."

His blue eyes crinkled at the corners. "Don't mention it. And you're not getting rid of me just yet. You'll need a hand to back your truck."

Before she could say she'd backed trucks for almost as

long as she'd ridden horses, he strode over to the fence and waited for her to swing the truck into position. She refused to look at him as she reversed. No matter what life threw at her she wasn't a helpless damsel in distress. She didn't need help. Period.

Despite her best intentions, she snuck a quick look as he waved at her to continue reversing. She'd seen plenty of attractive masculine profiles from her two years at Montana State University, there was no reason for blood to rush through her veins and render her light-headed. She really needed to eat.

"Whoa," he called out even as she applied the brakes.

Chin tilted, she quit the truck. Show time was over whether this man liked it or not. He needed to head to Marietta and then over the mountain pass to Bozeman to catch whatever chartered jet he'd arrived on.

From the corner of her eye, she caught a glimpse of charcoal-grey and white as he leaped over the wire fence. She swung around only to see that he'd thrown the canvas horse rug from the back of the truck over the barbed wire and that his jacket and tie now hung from the side of the truck.

She ground her teeth.

Just. Awesome.

The city-stranger had let the fresh air of the Big Sky Country get to him and now relived his Boy Scout days. He'd no idea what a dead weight a calf could be. It didn't matter if the fine weave of his white shirt stretched over the taut width of his back, his gym-honed muscles weren't built for country life. It would be her luck he'd pull a muscle and then how was she going to get him over the fence? Her other good friend, Trinity Redfern, might relish any opportunity to get up close and personal, but Payton had a ranch to run and no time to indulge her hormones.

"Thanks," she shouted, "I've got this." But the north wind stole her words.

Muttering beneath her breath, Payton let down the truck's tailgate. The capricious breeze whipped hair across her cheeks and lifted her lightweight dress. She muttered again, caught the hem before it made it past her thighs and tied a firm knot to ensure the full skirt wouldn't balloon upward again. She couldn't give Trinity back her impractical dress quick enough.

She turned to see the man heading her way. He'd rolled up the sleeves of his shirt and his strong arms easily carried the calf. His lips curved as he spoke soundless words of reassurance. The wind mussed his neat hair and his shirt gaped to reveal the tanned, strong column of his throat.

A fleeting memory teased her subconscious. The white flash of his smile reminded her of someone. But as he neared the fence and lifted the calf over the rug-covered wire and onto the tailgate, the memory fled. She took hold of the calf and eased him into the truck.

"Easy," she crooned as the calf struggled. She'd wrap the horse rug around his vulnerable body. She reached for the horse blanket on the fence at the same time as the stranger. Their hands tangled. Her eyes flew to his.

It didn't matter that he wore an expensive suit or drove a town rental car, she'd felt the calluses on his palms. She'd wager a new pair of boots. This man was no city-slicker.

He was a cowboy.

CORDELL MORGAN GAZED into thick-lashed eyes that he still couldn't decide were brown or gold. One minute they were the hue of an aspen leaf in the fall and the next they were chocolate-dark, like now.

Self-preservation told him to look the hell away. Nowhere in his five-year-plan did it include being intrigued by a woman who was as untamed and free-spirited as a wild mountain mustang.

She was slim-limbed to the point of fragility and her heavy, long brown hair framed delicate features. But she was more than a pretty face. Her direct gaze and the angle of her chin left him in no doubt her will was as strong and resolute as the granite embedded in the ground beneath his feet. The make-up and the girly cocktail dress didn't fool him. From the top of her windblown head to the toes of her scuffed boots she was a working cowgirl.

The calf struggled to its knees and as one they turned to make sure he didn't fall from the truck. With gentle words and efficient hands the woman tucked the horse rug around the calf and closed the tailgate.

She faced him and as the breeze toyed with her hair he caught the scent of fresh flowers. His jaw locked as he fought to keep his eyes on her face. The bodice of her strapless dress had slipped and now skimmed the tops of curves that would neatly fill his hands.

He reached for his jacket and tie and draped them over his arm. His testosterone could tantrum all it wanted, he had to leave. He'd already stayed too long if he noticed more about this cowgirl than the fact she had a calf needing mothering.

"Thanks again," she said with a sweet smile that reminded him of the sun's rays after a city winter's night. "I'll get going and take him to the ranch."

"A good feed of colostrum and he'll spark right up."

Her eyes searched his. "You haven't always been a cityboy, have you?"

He flexed his shoulders beneath the tailored shirt that, no matter how much it cost him, never felt comfortable.

"No."

There was no need to elaborate. But this unaffected woman would soon be nothing but a Montana memory and the knowledge loosened his tongue.

"No," he repeated, "I haven't. My twin brother and I grew up on a ranch outside Colorado Springs."

"It's a pretty part of the Rockies. Has your brother moved to the city too?"

Cordell shook his head. "The ranch wasn't big enough to support the two of us. He stayed and I moved away."

The cowgirl stood on tiptoes to reach into the truck and adjust the horse rug to better protect the calf from the wind. She spoke over her shoulder. "No wonder you're driving around sight-seeing while Eliza and Seth have their photographs, the mountain scenery would remind you of home."

He blanked out the way her dress inched a little higher up the cowgirl's smooth thighs. What was she talking about?

"I'm not driving around sight-seeing or even here to go to any wedding. I'm here on business."

She swung around, eyes dark and sharp. "You're here for business, not for today's wedding?"

"Yes." He looked toward the ranch buildings clustered on a distant hill.

She followed the direction of his gaze and folded her arms.

"If by business you mean you're going to see old Henry Watson, good luck. A century ago he'd have had run you out of town. He doesn't take kindly to strangers enquiring about his land."

Cordell didn't look away from the ranch dwarfed by the high-country backdrop. "So the stories are true?"

"It depends who's telling them. I only know him as a good and decent man." She inclined her head toward the pasture behind the truck. "This section isn't part of my ranch but Henry lets me use it because I'm all out of feed."

She paused and when she spoke again her tone had hardened. "He doesn't suffer fools easily. He also rightly doesn't see the fall he had last winter, or his lack of family, as grounds for an early retirement or a land grab. So, I'll give you some friendly advice. Cut your losses and return to town. The only way Henry will leave Larkspur Ridge Ranch is in a pine box."

Cordell slung his tie around his neck and shrugged on his suit coat. "Good advice but I'm not here to buy his land, I'm here to lease it."

"Lease?"

"Yes, Henry won't need to go anywhere and will have use of whatever land he wants. I'll then pay to use the rest. I've already spoken to him on the phone and he seemed agreeable in a terse, non-committal way. So I've come to meet with him face-to-face."

Her frown didn't ease. "There's other ranches for sale, why lease Larkspur Ridge when you could own another outright?"

He kept his expression neutral. This working cowgirl was as smart as a whip. He couldn't have her perceptive gaze pry free his secrets. "Larkspur Ridge is the right location and the right acreage. I also don't want to be locked into anything long-term. Unlike my brother, I ... like to move around."

"Fair enough." She glanced at the calf and unfolded her arms. "You know, you and Henry might get along. I've known him to wade into mud waist deep to rescue a calf.

And I'm also sure it will do him good to have some company." Her eyes sparkled pure gold. "Even if something tells me there will be times the two of you will butt heads."

She turned and leaned into the cabin of her truck. The skirt of her bunched dress hitched higher.

Mouth dry, Cordell glanced away. Never again would he look at a short pink hemline and not see long, shapely legs encased in cowboy boots.

"Here." She passed him a foil-covered dish. "Give him this to sweeten the deal. He loves his prime ribs and it might buy you five minutes before he shows you the door."

He accepted the plate. "Thanks. Who shall I say it's from?"

She held out her hand. "Payton ... Payton Hollis."

He covered her small hand in his. Her hand remained still and then her fingers curled around his. The warmth of her palm seeped into his bones.

"Cordell Morgan," he said, hoping his voice didn't emerge a husky rasp. Touching Payton left him as disorientated as a fall from a badass rodeo bull.

She nodded and slipped her hand free.

She turned before he could identify the emotion washing across her face and settled herself into the driver's seat. Her serious eyes met his through the open window. "Henry's a generous and honorable man; be straight with him and who knows, we might end up being neighbors."

Cordell watched until her rust-red pickup disappeared

over the gentle rise, a faint trail of bleached dust in its wake.

He strode toward his rental car. Neighbors or not, he wouldn't be seeing Payton Hollis again. Their paths couldn't cross. No matter how much he wished they could. The unspoilt cowgirl had caused something to unravel deep inside him and he needed his emotions to remain hog-tied. There was a reason why he never settled in one spot and kept his life entanglement free.

Just like there was a reason why leasing land wasn't the sole motive behind his coming to Marietta.

Chapter Two

THE PERSISTENT BARK of a black-and-white Australian Shepherd welcomed Cordell to Larkspur Ridge Ranch. He slowed on the graveled driveway as the Shepherd raced close to his wheels. The dog's instinct to herd might be invaluable out on the range but when it came to chasing cars it could become a liability. When he was sure the dog was again a safe distance away, he stopped and pulled on the emergency brake.

A double-story wooden building filled his windshield-framed view. While the ranch house had looked small and insignificant from the valley below, it now appeared as rugged and as stalwart as the mountains themselves. Movement drew his eye beyond the sprawling house and outbuildings to a corral where a buckskin mare paced. The dog's high-pitched barking intensified and the buckskin tossed her head, her black mane lifting in the wind.

Longing cut through Cordell like the lash of a bullwhip. What he wouldn't give to swap his suit for jeans and chaps and to throw a saddle on the restless horse. He understood how the corralled mare felt. Freedom was beyond both their grasps. He slid the silk knot of his tie into position. But he'd made his choices and now he had to live with them.

He tore his gaze away from the buckskin who held her head high, scenting the breeze coming off the snow-capped peaks. He might be the eldest by only a minute but it was his duty as the first-born son to look out for his twin brother. Serious and steady Ethan wasn't a risk-taker. He could spot a sick heifer a hundred yards away but he could no more head to the city to secure their financial future than the now tail-wagging dog could abandon its natural instincts.

Cordell opened the driver's side door and stood. The dog grinned and wriggled forward as though angling for a pat, except the Shepherd's bright eyes were centered on the foil-covered plate on the passage seat.

"You can't fool me," Cordell said with a chuckle as he bent to tickle behind the dog's silken ears. "It's not me you're overjoyed to see."

The dog dropped to the ground and rolled onto his back to expose the fluffy white underside of his belly. He rubbed the dog's stomach with the toe of his city-shoes. "And looking cute won't get me to slip you a rib. Payton would have my hide if I didn't deliver the whole plate to Henry."

Sensing, rather than hearing, someone approach, Cordell looked up. A tall, unsmiling, white-haired man stood a short distance away. Faded grey eyes locked with his. He went to remove his Stetson then remembered his felt hat lay packed in a box in his Denver condo. With a last rub to the dog's belly, he walked forward, his hand outstretched.

"Hello, Henry. I'm Cordell Morgan. We spoke over the phone."

The old man grunted, his fixed stare never wavering. Just when he thought Henry wouldn't shake his hand, the gnarled strength of the rancher's fingers grasped his. He concentrated on matching the power of Henry's handshake and on reading his face. The old rancher's craggy features may appear as if carved from stone but the laugh lines around his eyes and mouth spoke of a life well-lived. Payton had spoken the truth. Henry was a hard but decent man, a man to ride the river with.

A hint of acknowledgment softened Henry's gaze. Cordell hadn't been the only person making a snap character assessment.

The handshake ended and he lowered his arm. "Sorry I'm late. I stopped to help your neighbor Payton with a calf."

"You helped Payton?"

'Yes.'

Skepticism creased the old man's brow. "And she let you, just like that?"

"Actually, to be honest I didn't give her a choice. It didn't seem right her jumping over the fence in her dress, even if she had her boots on."

"So you jumped over in your suit instead?"

He shrugged. "As you do. I did take off my jacket and

tie."

A faint smile touched Henry's mouth. "As you do. And how did Payton take to you butting in?"

Cordell remembered the cuss words he couldn't hear but could see her lips form when he'd turned to make sure she didn't follow him. "Fine, considering she's used to doing things on her own."

"That she is. Anna and I weren't lucky to have children so Payton's the closest thing I have to a daughter. But even then, she's reluctant to accept help from me."

"Maybe I caught her in a soft moment but ..." Cordell swung away to retrieve the plate of prime ribs from the car. "She did wish me good luck and gave me these to buy five minutes of your time."

The dog's tail thumped on the gravel as he handed the plate to Henry.

The old man's eyes twinkled and Cordell had the impression he'd passed some sort of test before Henry's face resumed its impassive lines.

"Well then, you'd better come in."

Henry turned and for the first time Cordell realized his ramrod straight back belied a body twisted with age and pain.

He matched his stride to Henry's slower one as they walked toward the front doorsteps. From the corral a piercing whinny sounded.

Cordell stopped to gaze at the buckskin. He then glanced

back at Henry and noticed the old man had stopped too, but it was Cordell whom he examined and not the restless horse.

Henry inclined his head toward the buckskin. "Payton and I adopted this mare from the Pryor Mountain horse range. She's a mustang through and through and hasn't yet taken to her new home. I'm waiting for a truckload of hay to be delivered to Payton and then she'll go to Beargrass Hills. She'll be happier out of the corral."

Cordell nodded and erased all empathy for the mustang from his face. The man waiting for him held the reins of his future in his time-worn hands. He had a promise to keep and to do so he had to gain access to the lush pastures carpeting the rolling foothills below. But first he needed to get his act together. Payton had distracted him and now the mustang's yearnings continued to stir emotions he'd long ago buried.

Shoulders squared, he followed Henry up the steps, through the front door and down the hallway into the large kitchen filled with the pure mountain light. The huge windows, exposed beams and stone feature wall, all bespoke of an attention to detail and a desire to bring the natural beauty of Montana indoors. A light-fixture made from a circle of old lanterns hung over the table, but no homely knick-knacks or family photographs sat clustered on shelves. If a woman had lived here, her presence had long since faded.

"So," Henry said as he carefully settled himself into a

chair, "you'd better start talking, your five minutes starts now." He tousled the Australian Shepherd's head as the dog rested his head on his knee.

Cordell sat opposite Henry and leaned back in his chair. "I don't need to talk. You do. What do you want from a lease agreement?"

Respect glinted in Henry's slate-hard gaze. "You're a cool customer, aren't you?"

Cordell didn't answer. He wasn't going to waste time talking or feeling. He'd learned life's lessons all too well. Emotions were synonymous with weakness. To survive he couldn't allow himself to feel. No matter how high the stakes were.

"Let me see …" Henry stared out the windows to where the waning sunlight caught in the blue of the lake Cordell had passed on the drive in.

"I'm not leaving here until they carry me out. I don't want people poking their noses into my business. I like my peace and quiet too much to hire a ranch foreman and to fill the bunkhouse with strangers. I have more than enough money. I want to read and to fish. I want to see cattle grazing but don't want the responsibility." He paused, mouth tense. "I want to end my days with no regrets."

Cordell again remained silent, not wanting to intrude on the old rancher's memories as he continued to stare out the window as though lost in another time and place. As the silence swelled between them, he wasn't even sure if Henry remembered he was there. But when Henry's sharp gaze zeroed in on his, Cordell realized Henry knew exactly where he was and whom he was with.

"So if you can deliver on these things," he continued, his tone gruff, "you might have yourself a deal."

"I can. You'll have no regrets about leasing me your land."

"Maybe."

Henry rubbed at his thigh. Pain pinched his features.

"The pastures closest to Payton's ranch are off-limits. She has full use of them for as long as she needs."

Cordell nodded.

"*If* I let you have my land what will you use it for?"

"I've two truckloads of hungry cattle leaving Texas next week."

"Herefords?"

"No, black Angus."

"I'm not surprised they're hungry. Payton's part of the range might be dry but Texas is doing it real tough. The drought there just won't break."

"I know." The despair Cordell had witnessed when he'd visited Texas three weeks ago still kept him awake at night. "And it's not only the cattle suffering. If I could, I'd make it rain."

Desperation must have seeped into his words because Henry's eyes narrowed.

Cordell cleared his throat. If he had any chance of leasing

Larkspur Ridge Ranch he had to get himself under control. "So, I'll have my lawyer draw up a draft lease agreement and then –"

Henry came to his feet.

"Not so fast. This is far from a done deal." He looked at the foil-covered plate. "Rocky and I have some ribs to eat. See me tomorrow morning and I'll make my decision then."

Cordell pushed back his chair, using the simple movement to mask his tension. He'd lasted more than five seconds but he still had to pick his battles. He'd award round one to Henry but tomorrow there would be round two.

"No problem," he said as he too stood. "I'll come at nine."

"With some of Payton's chocolate-chip cookies."

"Sorry? Payton's cookies? I won't be seeing her again."

A ghost of a smile curved Henry's lips. "Where do you think you'll stay tonight?"

Cordell's tie suddenly choked like a silken noose. "Marietta? The woman at the rental car place at Bozeman said I didn't need to book ahead."

"Well, this weekend you do. Rosa, my housekeeper, says all the accommodation in town is booked out thanks to the wedding." Henry shuffled toward the kitchen door leading to the hallway signifying Cordell's time had more than expired. "Payton won't mind if you bunk in her bunkhouse. Beargrass Hills has plenty of beds since her dad ran it as a dude ranch."

Cordell followed Henry along the hallway. As Henry held open the front door, he briefly turned, mouth hard. "And if you don't want a black eye like that cowboy Rhett Dixon, remember Payton is only interested in one thing – her ranch."

"Easy there, buddy," Payton said as she lowered the bottle to reduce the milk flow to the hungry calf. She tightened her grip to make sure the calf didn't pull the plastic bottle from her grasp. It might have taken patience and persistence to encourage him to drink but once he got started there was no stopping him. She smiled at the expanding contours of his round belly. She'd like to see Cordell lift him now. The calf had almost drunk his own body weight in colostrum.

She glanced across the barn to where a black cow stared at them, her tail twitching. She hadn't liked being milked even though the action had reduced the pressure on her swollen udder. The cow had given birth to a stillborn heifer yesterday and Payton had brought her into the barn to make sure she caught any early signs of mastitis. As kind and as generous as Dr. Noah Sullivan was, she didn't need the expense of a vet bill should the cow's udder become inflamed. With any luck the cow would now accept the abandoned calf.

The little bull calf's sucking noises changed as the bottle emptied. She slipped the teat from his milk-frothed mouth.

He took a step toward her and then sank to the straw-covered floor before closing his eyes. She chuckled. Now he'd been fed the calf wouldn't be able to do anything but sleep. She'd wait until he grew hungry again and then she'd see if his new mother would let him suckle.

Bottle in hand, Payton left the barn. The evening breeze buffeted her and she dragged her denim jacket closed. It had felt so good to ditch the pink cocktail dress and pull on her faded jeans and warm blue plaid farm shirt. Fashionista Trinity would be horrified at her wardrobe choice but Payton dressed purely for practicality.

Payton's gaze strayed toward the high peaks that framed Henry's ranch house. Cordell had to be on his way to Marietta. She'd give him ten minutes tops before Henry would have sent him on his way. Her eyes lingered on the snow-crested slopes. The prospect of Cordell being gone shouldn't make her feel so ... empty. By his own admission he said he didn't stay in one place for too long. But there was just something about him that made a small, hidden part of her want a chance to get to know him better.

Was that dust on the road? She strained to see into the gloom and caught an unmistakable flash of silver. She swallowed. It was as though her thoughts had conjured Cordell out of the indigo shadows. From over near the kennel beneath the pine tree, Baxter barked and pulled at his chain confirming they'd soon have company. The liver-colored kelpie had been fed early and tied up to make sure he didn't spook either the cow or the calf.

Payton lifted a hand to her tangled hair, only to quickly lower it. What was she thinking? It didn't matter if her unspoken wish to see Cordell again had been granted or that she looked a mess. She had no room in her life for a man. But still her right hand sneaked to the backside of her worn jeans to check that the rip she'd torn when milking the uncooperative cow hadn't ripped further.

Cordell slowed and parked beside the barn. He dipped his head in greeting as he left the rental car. Despite the gathering chill, he'd discarded his jacket and tie. In the waning light, his white shirt accentuated the width of his shoulders and the honed contours of his chest. "Hey, Payton."

"Hey," she said, hoping her voice didn't betray how much her breathing had accelerated in the past three seconds. "The prime ribs seemed to have worked. You must have lasted at least five minutes."

Cordell stopped in front of her. The subtle scent of his aftershave teased her senses. He chuckled. "Yes, they did. Not that I was counting, but I would have been inside the ranch house for at least seven minutes."

The tightness constricting her chest intensified. His easy laugh was rich and genuine, with the power to stir yearnings she thought long dead.

"Wow. Henry was sociable." She searched Cordell's face for a sign of how their talk went but all she glimpsed was a deep weariness touched with a strange wariness. She arched a brow. "So ..."

"So ... I'm to come back tomorrow morning ... with some of your chocolate-chip cookies."

She shook her head. "He's such a rogue. Wait until I see him. You haven't just come for chocolate-chip cookies, have you? Let me guess, you need a place to stay?"

Seriousness dimmed the smile in his eyes. "Yes. If it was no trouble. Henry said Marietta would be booked out with wedding guests." He glanced toward the large tin-roofed building to his left. "And he assured me you have plenty of beds."

She hesitated. "I do ... it's just the bunkhouse has no running water. My foreman and his wife left yesterday to visit their daughter and I swear as soon as they drove through the main gate the windmill stopped. The bunkhouse water tank is bone dry so there's no chance of you taking a shower." She fought the heat sweeping into her cheeks at the sudden image of water sluicing over the hard-packed torso only an arm's length away. "There are plenty of beds inside if you don't mind a room with floral wallpaper, carpet and drapes. My mom had a thing for flowers."

"Thanks. I wasn't looking forward to sleeping in my car." The corner of his mouth curled in a smile. "I'm secure with my masculinity, I think I can handle a flower or too."

Her own lips twitched. "Well, that's good to hear. Luckily for you, Maria also left a freezer full of food, otherwise grilled cheese sandwiches would be the only item on the dinner menu."

"It's sleep not food I need, so a grilled cheese sandwich actually sounds pretty good. I don't want you to run short of meals."

"It's fine. Trust me. You'd much rather eat Maria's food. Even Baxter thinks twice before scoffing my meat loaf. Maria and Joe might be away for a fortnight but she's left me enough meals for a month."

Cordell nodded before his gaze dropped to the forgotten bottle in her hand. "How's the calf?"

"Good. When he's ready for his next feed I'll see if the cow that lost her calf yesterday will let him suckle. And if she doesn't I'll try the Vicks trick."

"I know the Vicks trick well. The strong smell will mask the scent of an unfamiliar calf. Your mother might have liked flowers but mine liked Vicks." Cordell pulled face. "Both for abandoned calves and sick boys."

Payton's laughter filled the small space between them. For a brief moment the weight of responsibility and the desperate need for rain didn't press so hard on her shoulders.

"I take it you didn't get a cold or the flu often?"

"No. And our cat soon stopped scratching the lounge. It seems Vicks has uses only my mother knew about." Cordell glanced toward the closed barn door. "Ethan actually uses another trick to re-mother his calves. He wets the calf and covers it in grain. After a night spent licking the feed off the calf, by morning the cow has then bonded with her new baby."

"What a great idea. Perhaps my Vicks days will be over too. I'll try it tonight if Miss-Cranky-Pants won't play nice with the small bundle of cuteness I just fed."

He smiled. "If you need a hand, let me know."

"Thanks, I'll be fine. You'll need your beauty sleep if you're to face Henry tomorrow."

"Well, if you change your mind, you'll know where I'll be. I'll grab my bag and follow you inside."

She nodded and made her way over to where Baxter lay, his head on his paws and bright eyes never leaving Cordell. She unfastened the chain from his red leather collar. He bolted over toward their guest. She didn't whistle him to her side. Cordell would cope with Baxter licking him to death.

She tucked the milk bottle under her arm and headed toward the front porch of the single-story ranch house. The desert areas of Montana would ice over before she'd change her mind about Cordell helping her with the calf. And she didn't need any reminder about where he'd be. Her stomach did a strange little flip.

He'd be three doors down the hall.

Chapter Three

PAYTON SMOTHERED A yawn and worked quickly to fill the plastic calf bottle with the last of the colostrum. After dinner Cordell had spent an hour on the phone before he'd gone to take a shower. She needed to get to the barn before he decided to help her with the calf and before she heard the sound of running water in the guest bathroom. Her hormones already fixated on the fact Cordell would soon be naked.

She pulled the rubber calf teat onto the bottle. Her cheeks radiated as much warmth as the cooker on which she'd heated the milk. For some reason sitting across the table at dinner in the small, cozy kitchen from a smiling Cordell had raised her body's core temperature. And it hadn't yet subsided. She dragged her unruly hair off her face. She needed to get back to reality. She had a ranch to run and a drought to survive. Remaining hyper-aware of Cordell, no matter how gorgeous he was, wasn't going to get her chores done. Her teenage-crush days had ended a lifetime ago back in high school.

She collected the bottle, strode along the hall to the mudroom where she collected her worn denim jacket from off the coat rack. What had Henry been thinking suggesting Cordell bunk with her? He probably thought Cordell would at least be safe around her. It was common knowledge Payton coped just fine on her own. Even if blue-eyed cowboys like Rhett Dixon were determined to challenge her independence and single-status.

She set the bottle on the floor. The upside of Cordell's visit was that he'd only stay a night. A night that was at least a third of the way through. Come morning her life would resume its safe, solitary and predictable routine. She shrugged on her coat and pulled her too-long hair out from beneath the collar. One of these days she was going to have to sit still for Mandy to give her a quick trim. A floorboard behind Payton creaked. She swung around. She'd left making her escape too late.

"Sorry," Cordell said with a weary grin. "I didn't mean to surprise you."

"It's fine." She frowned. "I thought you were taking a shower."

He nodded. "I didn't want to waste your water, so I kept it short."

As he stepped closer she could see his damp hair. He was dressed in a simple grey T-shirt and dark denim jeans and his feet were bare. Her frown deepened as the clean scent of soap filled her lungs. She needed to get out more. She never knew a man could smell so good. Or that the tight stretch of a cotton T-shirt could empty her head of all rational thought.

"Thanks. I appreciate it." She bent to pick up the milk bottle. "Water is like liquid gold around here at the moment." She inclined her head toward the kitchen. "There's coffee in the pot. Make yourself at home. I'll be in the barn a while if the cow's temper hasn't improved."

"Wait. I'll grab my shoes and come too," he said as he turned to retrace his steps.

"No, you don't have to —"

But like at the roadside, Cordell appeared to have selective hearing and disappeared down the hallway. She stomped her feet into her boots.

Cordell soon joined her, his mirror-polished shoes looking out of place with his jeans.

She planted her hands on her hips. 'Thanks, but I really don't need any help.'

"I know." His lips curved. "I'm not coming to help, I'm coming to watch."

"Watch?"

"Yes. My money's on the cow if you try to milk her again."

"And why would you think I can't handle one grouchy cow?"

Laughter gleamed in the blue of his eyes. "Because the back of your jeans tells me you've landed on your butt more than once this afternoon."

She failed to catch her own smile. She'd checked the state of the rip but hadn't dusted off the seat of her jeans. Several well-timed kicks from the unimpressed cow had sent her butt-first onto the dusty barn floor.

"Okay. Yes. There were a few pecking-order issues but it will all be fine now. Besides, the cow might accept the calf and I won't have to milk her."

Cordell headed for the door. "Let's go and find out."

"You know your fancy city shoes will get trashed in the barn," she called after him. But as her gaze slid from his broad shoulders, down to his Wrangler-clad butt, all reasons why he should stay inside fled. Muttering beneath her breath, she grabbed her father's old sheepskin coat and followed Cordell out into the darkness.

"Here, put this on," she said as they reached the red barn door. The coat wasn't so much to warm Cordell against the night air but for her piece of mind. Something had to be wrong with her? Lean, long-legged cowboys were nothing new in her world, so why did this cowboy's smile have the power to make her breath hitch?

She handed him the coat. She didn't need to be distracted by the flex of a smooth biceps. She wasn't landing back on her butt on the barn floor around Cordell anytime soon.

"Thanks."

His white grin flashed in the moonlight as he slid on the jacket.

She opened the barn door and switched on the barn light

that would illuminate the entrance and leave the pens shadowed. The rustle of straw sounded as the cow stood and turned to look at them.

Payton entered the calf's pen and ran a hand along his soft black back. He blinked his wide eyes open to stare at her. She'd take the edge off his hunger before she let him loose on the cow's full and tender udder.

"Hey buddy, it's dinner time."

The calf scrambled to his feet and head-butted her knees looking for milk. She guided the teat into the calf's mouth. When he sucked strongly, she glanced toward the still quiet cow and then to where Cordell leaned his hip against the wooden pen rail.

"Sorry to disappoint you but there could be no show," she said with a grin. "Miss-Cranky-Pants over there is half asleep and appears quite amiable. She might adopt the calf without a fuss and then I won't have to milk her."

The corner of Cordell's mouth kicked into a half-mile. "Or she's lulling you into a false sense of security."

"Thanks. You're a regular ray of sunshine."

His rich laughter rippled through the fine hairs on her nape. He moved away from the wooden rail. "How about I go and find some grain for our Plan A. There looks to be feed bins over there to the right?"

She nodded, her attention diverted as the impatient calf butted the bottle wanting a quicker milk flow.

Cordell returned with a grain-filled bucket.

"He's a lucky little critter. I was in Texas a few weeks ago and a calf like him wouldn't have stood a chance. Cow's didn't have the strength to stand let alone milk for a newborn."

"That's dreadful." Her eyes lingered on Cordell's drawn features. The rawness of his words hinted at a fatigue that bit deeper than physical exhaustion.

Cordell stared at the calf. "That's why I need Henry's land. He hasn't run cattle for years and pasture-rich Larkspur Ridge is a hungry Texan cow's idea of paradise."

"So you've bought some cattle to fatten?"

She again concentrated on feeding the calf. Cattle-trading was a common ranch practice but it didn't feel quite right Cordell making money off someone else's misfortune. He would have purchased the starving cattle for a pittance and would make a healthy profit once they grew sleek and fat.

"I haven't bought them. I'm helping out an old friend." Cordell paused. "Luke gave me a place to stay when I needed one and it's the least I can do to save the last of his breeding stock. His family has bred cattle for four generations and the financial pressure of no rain has cost him his marriage. I now can't let him lose everything. I said I'd take care of the cattle until he got back on his feet."

From the gravity of Cordell's words she knew such a thing could take a while even if rain were to fall across the Lone Star State.

"This little critter might be lucky, but your friend is lucky too; he has you."

"Maybe." Cordell rubbed a hand along his jaw. "He swears his grey hair is a result of all the things I dragged him into when we were youngsters on the rodeo circuit."

"Boys will be boys."

Cordell smiled but even in the poor light she could see his smile didn't reach his eyes. "Some boys took more risks than others. My Denver agricultural consultancy business can run itself for a while. I owe it to Luke to get my hands dirty and to safeguard his, and his infant son's, future."

The calf sucked the last of the milk from the bottle, his appetite in no way satisfied.

"Okay," she said as she opened the wooden pen gate and slipped through before the calf could follow her. "Let's see if your brother's trick works. Do your water and grain thing and we'll introduce the cow to her new, beautiful baby."

"Please tell me I'm not seeing things," Payton said the next morning from the barn doorway. Cordell turned away from the sight of the calf feeding from the contented cow. He narrowed his eyes as the bright early morning light poured through the door Payton had left open behind her.

"No, you're not. Your cranky cow has turned into a doting mother."

"My Vicks days are behind me. The grain trick really

works," Payton said as she rested her arms beside his on the top timber rail of the cow's pen. He breathed in her sweet floral scent and felt the companionable pressure of her arm against his. "Look at his little tail wiggle, he's so happy, and look at the size of his belly. He can't possibly be hungry any more."

Cordell only nodded. He needed another second or two before he could speak. The beauty of Payton's smile delivered such a jolt to his senses he knew the water and grain plan was the only thing to have worked. He'd thought a sleepless night would blur the effect this Montana cowgirl had on him. His jaw clenched. He'd been wrong. Her happiness danced through him like the dust swirling through the streams of barn light.

"Your brother is one clever cowboy."

"Yes, he is."

She was so close he could see the thick length of her dark lashes, the satin hue of her skin and the natural pink of her full lips. Her hair was pulled back into a ponytail and her fine-boned face was all high cheekbones and large eyes. But as fragile as she appeared, the strength of her spirit shone from her intelligent brown gaze.

He straightened so their arms no longer touched. He had to get out of the barn and away from all temptation to tug her close and explore the soft skin below her jawline with his mouth. He'd come to Montana to lease Henry's land and to make peace with the past. Not to have his self-control desert him.

He forced himself to remain still while she reached out to touch his jacket collar. When she lowered her arm he saw straw caught between her fingers.

"Did you sleep here?"

He stiffened. He'd hoped she wouldn't discover where he'd spent the night. The knowledge would only lead to questions he didn't want to answer.

"Yes." He forced a casual smile. "I lied when I said I could handle sleeping in a room full of flowers."

"But I came in at one and again at four and you weren't here?"

"I was. You brought a flashlight. I didn't want to scare you or talk in case I spooked the cow."

"You slept here *all* night?" she said frowning at a pen filled with clean straw.

"And it was quite comfortable compared to some of the places I've slept on the rodeo circuit."

"But why stay? You were dog-tired and I had everything under control."

"I know you did." He scraped a hand through his city-short hair. "I couldn't sleep so thought I may as well be on hand if the cow didn't share your view of the calf being cute enough to be her own."

Her frown cleared but the intensity of her stare didn't waver.

"Thank you."

"You're welcome."

"Do you often not sleep?"

"It depends on where I am." He swung away toward the open barn door. His secrets, along with his emotions, had to remain hidden. "I don't know about you, but I hear the coffee pot calling."

He stepped into the new day and strode toward the ranch house. But as fast as he moved he couldn't outrun the darkness of the memories that stalked his dreams no matter where he slept.

TWO COFFEES LATER, Cordell drove through the wooden archway of the Larkspur Ridge main gate. Heavy dew clung to the gossamer cobwebs strung between the wire of the fence either side of the road. Behind him pockets of mist lazed in the valley hollows. Winter would soon throw its blanket of white over the mountains but Henry's land would provide perfect wintertime grazing. The draws and gullies would offer protection from the snow and the pine trees respite from the wind. The Texan cattle would soon grow thick coats and adapt to their new environment.

He swallowed. If only he could be so resilient. The knot in his gut told him he could stay at Payton's ranch countless winters and still his self-control would hemorrhage. Never before had he found it so difficult to remain on task or to keep his feelings in check when around a woman. It wasn't just how she looked. Sure her smile kicked him harder than a stallion's hoof, but she was so much more than a beautiful face. Her strength, her kindness and her generosity humbled him.

She'd insisted he wear her father's sheepskin jacket to see Henry. She argued that Henry would relate to him more than if he wore his suit. Cordell's grip firmed on the steering wheel. But when he then returned the jacket, his visit to Beargrass Hills would have to be his last. Even if Henry agreed to the lease proposition and he and Payton became neighbors, he had to put distance between them before he forgot who he was and why he'd come to Montana. Once Luke's cattle were settled, Cordell could split his time between Marietta and Denver until the pieces of his friend's life slotted back together.

He approached the ranch house and just like before, Rocky dashed toward the rental car. But this time, a shrill whistle sounded and the Australian Shepherd retraced his steps to where Henry hobbled away from the corral. Behind him the buckskin had her nose deep in the bucket of food Henry had delivered.

Cordell parked the sedan, collected Payton's container of chocolate-chip cookies and made his way over to the old rancher. The buckskin lifted her head, her nostrils flaring, before returning to her feed.

Henry eyed off Cordell's mismatched city-shoes, jeans and sheepskin jacket. "Coat Payton's idea?" A suspicion of a smile warmed his grey gaze.

"Yup. The things I do to get you your cookies. It was no coat, no cookies."

Cordell bent to rub the Shepherd's ears. "Sorry, no ribs today, Rocky."

"For someone who slept in a bed you look like hell," Henry said as Cordell carefully straightened, "and you move like you're as old as me."

He rolled his bad shoulder. He'd once come off second-best riding a black bronc that was more devil than horse.

"We re-mothered the calf last night, so I slept in the barn."

Henry grunted, the brief dip of his head telling Cordell that the sound was more one of approval than disinterest. "Did you use Vicks?"

"No, grain and water. My brother swears by it."

Henry's eyes narrowed.

"Smart man. Younger brother?"

"Yes, by minutes."

"That figures. Identical twins?"

"No. But we do look similar even if we are then very different."

"Let me guess." Henry's stare zeroed in on Cordell's stiff shoulder. "He's not so knocked about?"

Cordell grinned. "True. But while I might have a few more aches and pains than Ethan, there's plenty of life left in me yet. I could still go a bareback bronc round or two."

Henry chuckled. "You and me both."

The old rancher's laughter shaved decades off his face. The rigid line of his jaw relaxed as memories returned him to an earlier life. Cordell's own rodeo memories stirred. The smell of leather, dust and sweat. The intense quiet as the chute opened. The rush of adrenaline as the horse beneath him exploded into life.

A gust of cold wind funneled down the back of his neck and returned him to the present. There were no more rodeos. Just promises to keep. He adjusted the sheepskin coat collar. "Henry," he said, voice now quiet, "I know what you're up to. It won't work."

An indefinable expression flashed across his weathered face, before his mouth tensed. "And what's that?"

"Payton is like a daughter to you and so it's only natural you want to help her."

"That might be so but we both know that Payton accepting help is as likely as a blizzard in summer."

"But it doesn't stop you ... and me ... from trying. You delayed making your decision last night so I'd stay with her, didn't you?"

Henry's only answer was a scowl that would have sent a lesser man hightailing it to his car.

Cordell held his sub-zero gaze. He'd dealt with men far frostier than Henry. "I agree, in a perfect world Payton wouldn't be on her own and responsible for running Beargrass Hills. But I'm not the answer. The truth is I'm no good for her." He swallowed past an unexpected sense of loss. "I have trouble staying in one place and she needs someone steady and reliable like my brother."

"She doesn't need someone like your brother. She needs someone who understands her. Someone who will risk everything for her." Henry rubbed at his thigh and inclined his head toward the valley to their right now bathed in the bright morning light. "Walk with me."

Cordell nodded and walked beside him, matching his slow pace. What had he been thinking bringing Payton into the conversation? Sleep deprivation was no excuse for acting on the impulse to make sure Henry didn't send any more would-be suitors in Payton's direction. Losing focus and allowing his emotions to sidetrack him wasn't going secure him the land that now rolled before him in a sea of wind-blown green.

Henry stopped at the edge of the driveway and together they stared out at the empty pastures dotted with pine trees instead of glossy-coated cattle.

"The land's yours," Henry said in a husky voice, without looking at him.

Cordell remained silent for a moment. "Just like that?"

"Yup." Still Henry didn't make eye contact. "Take it or leave it."

"I'll take it."

A smile touched Henry's mouth as he turned toward him.

"I thought so. There's two conditions."

"Name them."

"Payton's chocolate-chip cookies."

He handed the container of cookies to Henry. "And?" He clenched his teeth. He already knew what was coming.

"There's an old cabin but it's inhabitable. The quickest way in, apart from through here, is the gate you passed on your way from Payton's."

"So when I return in a week, you want me to stay at Beargrass Hills Ranch?"

"Yes and I want you to pay board. Payton needs the money. She has a heart as generous as her mother's so she'll refuse to accept payment but I'm counting on you to make sure she takes it."

"Done." He matched Henry's brusque tone. "But I'm putting it on record that it doesn't matter how much time we spend together, I won't ever be right for Payton."

"Maybe and maybe not. One person who isn't right for her is Rhett Dixon." Henry shook his head. "Now there's a set of twins that couldn't be more different. Rhett could do with some of his twin sister's sense. Kendall's just as worried about their sick mother but she knows better than to hang around those troublesome Taylor boys." Henry paused and held out his hand. "So shall I expect to hear from your city-lawyer this afternoon?"

Cordell shook Henry's hand. "Yes, I'll call him on my way out."

But as his arm lowered to his side and he gazed out at the foothills that were now his, unease shouldered aside his relief. He'd secured the land he needed but at a price.

He'd be living with the one woman he had to stay away from.

Chapter Four

"Now *that's what* I'm talking about," Trinity said, her words ending in a drawn-out sigh.

Payton didn't have to look up from scanning the rodeo program to know her friend salivated over a man. Trinity had only come to the 76th Copper Mountain Rodeo for one thing – cowboys. Luckily Payton had come for the events. She read the list once again. She'd run late helping a cow calve and if Trinity and Mandy didn't stop dawdling to look at the masculine scenery they'd never make it to the main arena to catch the tie-down roping.

"I hear you," Mandy replied from Payton's left, a dreamy note in her voice. "Come on Pay, take a look. You can't be all work and no play. The view will make your day."

Payton sighed. She'd have no peace until she threw a token glance toward the cowboy. She looked up from the program. "You guys, the only thing that will make –" Her jaw dropped.

The cowboy, dressed in jeans, chaps and a blue western shirt, who tied a black horse to the side of a trailer was the last person she'd expected to see.

Cordell.

Mandy giggled. "Trinity, mark this day. Payton's mouth is hanging open and she isn't checking out a nice piece of horseflesh. Eliza might be on the other side of the world honeymooning in Australia, but I'm going to have to call her."

Cheeks burning, Payton snapped her mouth shut. "No, you don't. Leave Eliza and Seth in peace. It's not what you think."

"So tell us what it is like, then," Mandy said with a raised fine brow.

"That's Cordell."

"You *know* him?" Trinity asked, green eyes round. "Because I can guarantee he's not from around here."

"He's not. That's the cowboy leasing Henry's land."

Mandy grabbed her arm. "The one *staying* with you."

"Yes. Three doors down the hall."

"We are so having a girls' night in at your place," Mandy said. "How does next Friday sound?"

Payton laughed. "No way. I'm not sitting through one of those chick flicks with you again. But I might consider cooking dinner one night if you let go of my arm before I lose all feeling in my fingers."

"Sorry," Mandy said with an unrepentant grin, releasing her. "I can't believe you were holding out on us."

"I wasn't. I told you about him."

"You did, but you left out a few important details." The laughter in Trinity's eyes dimmed. "He might look good in his Wrangler jeans but is he a good guy? You shouldn't be out there alone with him, if he isn't. When are Joe and Maria back?"

"Joe and Maria won't be back for another week but it's fine, Trin. I can take care of myself. And, yes, he's a good guy. I wasn't expecting him for a couple more days. I guess that's why I looked … surprised."

A dimple flickered in Trinity's cheek as she smiled. "Yes, the expression on your face was pure … surprise."

"Don't look now," Mandy said, "but your gorgeous, good guy is staring at us."

"He's not my guy. You both know I've only time for my ranch." Despite her words, fresh heat surged in her face as Cordell lifted a hand in a brief wave. "Now you two, behave," she warned as he strode toward them.

Cordell's smiling blue eyes touched each of them in greeting before he doffed his felt hat at her. "Payton."

"Hi." She quickly spoke, even knowing her voice would emerge far too high. She was pretty sure Trinity and Mandy, for once, would be speechless. A man shouldn't look so damn fine.

"Cordell, these are my good friends, Trinity," Payton inclined her head toward the smiling brunette on her right, and then toward the beaming blonde to her left, "and Mandy."

"It's nice to meet you both." He smiled a crooked grin. "Great job getting Payton off the ranch and away from her cows."

"Hey, I like my cows."

But her words were lost beneath Trinity's and Mandy's breathless giggles.

Just. Perfect. Her two besties were already besotted. And they hadn't even seen what Cordell looked like on a horse yet.

Trinity cast an eye over Payton's conservative small belt buckle and her plainly stitched boots. "We're still working on her wardrobe but we are making progress. She wore a dress last weekend."

Cordell's mouth curved. "I know."

The dark flash of appreciation in his eyes caused Payton's toes to curl.

She silenced a groan as Trinity's and Mandy's bright and curious gazes centered on her. As soon as they were alone, Payton would be in for a grilling. There were a few details about Cordell she hadn't yet mentioned, least of all how they'd met and what she'd worn.

"So," she said, tone firm trying to regain control of the conversation, "what brings you to the 76th Copper Mountain Rodeo? I didn't think you were due in town for another day or so."

'I wasn't but seeing as I'll be working cattle soon I thought I'd freshen up my roping skills." He paused. "I did leave a message on your ranch phone. I don't have your cell number."

"Sorry, with Maria away I keep forgetting to check for messages."

"No problem, I only expected a call if it didn't suit for me to arrive today."

She nodded and forced herself to hold his gaze. She'd forgotten how crystal clear his blue eyes were and how strong the line of his jaw. Her fingers had the sudden urge to trace the stubble-blurred curve from his chin to his mouth. She jammed her hands into her jeans pockets and forced her breathing to slow. She'd soon have some explaining to do. Her friends would know when she was flustered. And when it came to the cowboy in front of her, all he seemed to do was upset her rock-steady equilibrium.

Trinity looped her arm through Mandy's and pulled her away from Payton's side.

"Nice to meet you, Cordell," she said, "good luck in the tie-down roping. We'll make sure we cheer for you." Trinity glanced at Payton, her eyes innocent. "Mandy and I need to catch up with Selah over there and we'll meet you in the stands."

Then before she could even assemble the words, "I'm coming with you," Trinity and Mandy had walked away.

Payton looked back at Cordell and found his intent gaze on her.

She wet her dry lips. At least her precious cows never left

her alone with a cowboy whose smile scrambled her thoughts. Wait until she saw Trinity and Mandy. They'd already caught up with dark-haired Selah Davis as they'd been talking to the gorgeous Seattle journalist when Payton had arrived. Selah had returned to cover the rodeo for her women's magazine, Charisma.

"How's the calf doing?" Cordell asked, voice low and casual.

"Good, thanks." Then realizing her reply sounded far too formal, she smiled. "You won't believe how much he's grown."

"I bet he has. He was a greedy little critter."

Cordell's words were warm but still a strange seriousness tempered his gaze. It was as though he was as uncertain as she was about being alone with her. Get real. Cordell might not stay around for long but when it came to women his cowboy swagger and grin would leave a trail of languishing hearts behind.

She searched for something to say. "When are you expecting Luke's cattle?"

"In two days. That will give me a chance to check Henry's fences and water." His eyes examined hers. "Are you sure it's okay me arriving early?"

She ensured her expression remained neutral. She'd counted on the extra days to make sure her self-control would be watertight. But if her earlier open-mouthed reaction at seeing him was any indication she'd have needed extra weeks.

When Cordell had returned her father's sheepskin jacket and asked if he could bunk with her while he leased Henry's land, she'd agreed. Her self-preservation had hyper-ventilated at the thought of him staying longer than one night but Beargrass Hills Ranch was the logical location to base himself. The starving cattle would need attention and time and Cordell would be close enough to provide both.

"It's fine. You'll just have to suffer my cooking and sleeping in the main house until Maria and Joe are back next week. Joe can then tinker with the windmill so there'll be running water at the bunkhouse again."

"Sounds like a good plan. I'll be coming and going at all hours and so won't disturb you over there. But you don't need to cook for me while I'm in the main house. I'll take care of myself."

She frowned. "That doesn't seem fair. I feel bad enough as it is about accepting money for having you stay. How about if you cook, you don't pay board?"

Cordell's jaw hardened. "We went over this before I left. I'm staying and so I'll pay."

She slipped her hands from out of her jeans pockets. Now she was on familiar ground and in her comfort zone. Arguing with a strong-willed cowboy she could handle. It was the uncertainty and confusion she felt around him that ruined her composure.

"Actually, I don't think we resolved our earlier discussion."

"Yes. We did. I'm paying."

A horse's impatient whinny punctuated his words.

Cordell turned to look at his trailer.

"That would be His Lordship telling me to get a move on. I'd best get him saddled and warmed up."

"Outside the main arena there's a smaller space where you can put him through his paces."

"Thanks." Cordell pushed his hat brim a little higher so their eyes could fully meet. "Listen Payton, you know I have to pay, as well as stay. That was part of Henry's conditions to lease his land."

"I know, as I said before he's such a rogue. Thank you again for being honest with me." She sighed. "I still don't feel comfortable about you paying but I concede defeat ... this time."

"MOSSY, STOP LOOKING at me like that," Cordell said as he approached his restless horse. "Yes, I talked to Payton for too long. And yes, I need to stay away from her."

Mossy's ears flattened and he aimed a kick at Cordell that would have hit a fly on a wall. He automatically sidestepped Mossy's hoof. The horse's show of bad temper was nothing but a game, a game that could still leave him bruised if he didn't keep his wits about him.

He collected Mossy's saddle blanket and saddle from inside the trailer. And it wouldn't only be Mossy's teeth or hooves that would pack a wallop if he didn't concentrate. His own conscience would give him a hiding if he lost sight of why he'd come to Marietta. The five days away from Montana had in no way diluted his response to Payton.

When her friends had left the two of them alone, he'd been strangely tongued-tied. For a man never lost for words, all it took was tousled brown hair and the tight hug of faded denim and he was as incoherent as a schoolboy. And it had to stop. Once at Beargrass Hills he'd keep himself so busy their paths wouldn't cross. Thanks to old Henry, they might be living in close proximity but he'd meant what he'd said that Payton deserved better than him.

He exited the trailer, saddle blanket and saddle slung over his arm. Hooves drummed to his left and he swung around. Rodeos would test an anxious horse. The crackle of the loudspeaker or the squeal of an excited child could all trigger a horse's instinct to run.

He tensed as he caught sight of a riderless bay galloping toward him. Stirrups flapping and reins dragging, the horse ducked and weaved through the thin crowd as he headed for the open space of where the trailers congregated. Cordell dumped the saddle, reached into the trailer to grab Mossy's half-full feed bucket and glanced in the direction Payton had walked. His mouth dried. She stood talking to Henry near a goose-neck trailer, both of their backs toward the runaway horse.

A scream sounded. He high-tailed it over to the dirt road along which the horse travelled. A young mother, a chubby baby on her hip, abandoned the pram she was pushing to run behind a trailer as the horse bore down on them. The horse clipped the navy pram as he sped by and it toppled over.

Cordell stepped onto the road, making sure he didn't fully block the frightened horse's escape route. Talking softly he called to the bay, held out the bucket and then shook it so the rattle of grain sounded. The horse didn't slow or appear to notice him standing there. Cordell remained where he was. Shoulders relaxed and voice calm, he continued to call to the horse and shake the bucket. Just when he thought the bay would race past, the gelding swung around to face him and pulled to a jarring stop. Head high, he snorted, his sweat-darkened flanks quivering.

"Steady boy," Cordell crooned.

The horse took one and then two steps toward him and sank his nose into the bucket. He snatched a mouthful of grain and then flung up his head. Knowing one sudden move or sound would spook the horse, Cordell remained still. The horse again snorted and lowered his head to the grain. The bay took a step closer and this time he didn't lift his head as he ate.

Cordell touched the hot and damp skin of the horse's neck and eased his hand forward to secure the loose reins.

Boots pounded on the ground and Cordell shook his

head to stop a white-faced youth from rushing over to the horse.

"It's okay," he said gently, "give him a little longer to settle."

The youth nodded and bent to rest his elbows on his knees to catch his breath.

When satisfied the horse wasn't going to bolt, Cordell led him over to the youth who accepted the reins with a shaky smile. "Thanks so much. It's his first rodeo and a kid popped a balloon near him."

"I thought so," Cordell said with a smile, "he's just a young un'. Go easy with him past those flags."

He watched the gelding walk behind his owner as they headed toward two flags attached to the arena fence and that fluttered high above the trailers. As the gelding shied sideways, a tall, well-built cowboy came to the youth's side and took hold of the horse's reins.

Cordell caught the youth's relieved, "Thanks, Levi," before he turned away to carry the feed bucket over to his trailer and continue to saddle Mossy.

PAYTON DIDN'T KNOW where to look. Palms cold, she glanced over to where Cordell was saddling his horse as if nothing had happened. Beside her, Henry stared at the toppled pram, his shoulders bowed and his face pale beneath his tan.

She touched his arm. "Henry, there was no baby in the pram, remember? We thought there was and then we saw the mother carrying the baby behind the trailer."

Henry nodded, but the tension etching his face in sharp and strained lines didn't lessen. Anna and Henry had never been blessed with children and Henry had a soft spot for calves and foals. Seeing the pram tip over and for a brief time assuming a baby had been inside, had scared him. And he wasn't the only one.

She willed her heart to stop racing. It hadn't only been a possible baby in the pram whom she'd felt fear for.

"What was Cordell thinking?" she muttered through clenched teeth.

Henry cleared his throat beside her. "He was always going to be okay. He has a way with horses."

"A way with horses? I'd call it a death wish. I mean who steps out in front of a runaway horse like that?"

"Pay, he wasn't right in front of the horse. It just looked like he was from this angle."

Anger trembled in her hands. "I don't care where he stood. He could have been … hurt."

She stopped talking before she said, and revealed, too much.

"He's survived the rodeo circuit and that black horse of his isn't one I'd turn my back on, he knows what he's doing."

As she watched, Cordell's horse bared its teeth at him as

he tightened his girth. Cordell didn't flinch or move away. The horse snapped on air and then faced forward. Cordell gently pulled the horse's front legs to make sure the girth didn't pinch, before gathering the reins and swinging into the saddle.

Her anger drained away like water through the desert-dry earth of her ranch.

Okay. Trinity's and Mandy's admiration wasn't misplaced. She'd now seen Cordell on a horse. And yes, he looked as good on horseback as he did standing on the ground wearing boots, snug jeans and leather chaps.

She glanced at Henry who also was watching Cordell. Color hadn't yet returned to the old rancher's face.

"He might have had everything under control with the horse," she said, "but you can't tell me Cordell doesn't take unnecessary risks."

A twinkle returned to Henry's faded grey gaze. "I know a certain cowgirl who also takes unnecessary risks instead of asking for help and who has adopted a mountain mustang who isn't exactly as quiet as a lamb."

She returned Henry's smile. "*We* adopted the mustang and I'm not even going to start on what risky things you do that your doctor has told you that you shouldn't."

The loudspeaker crackled into life announcing the tie-down roping would soon commence.

She glanced toward the main arena. "I'd best get going before all the action starts without me."

Henry's expression sobered. "Pay, why aren't you competing? The ladies' barrel-race has always been your event and you missed it last year for the 75th Copper Mountain Rodeo anniversary as well."

She pressed a kiss to his weathered cheek. "Too busy."

The truth was she had even less money this year to enter or to run her trailer into town, but that wasn't Henry's concern.

"Next year," she added with a smile that she hoped covered her fears.

She headed toward the main arena and lifted her hat to drag her hand through her hair. Surely by the 77th Copper Mountain Rodeo it would have rained. Surely by next year she'd be making good on her graveside promise to her parents that their only child would never let them down.

Chapter Five

"So ...?"

As she'd been doing since she'd joined her friends on the bleachers, Payton ignored Mandy's loaded question. Before the tie-down roping had started she'd given them enough information about when she'd met Cordell but left out all the parts to do with how he made her feel so out of control. Especially when he took dangerous risks.

She'd even disappeared to buy popcorn, hoping it would keep her friends silent. The loudspeaker boomed introducing the next competitor for the rope and tie event.

"Who hoo, Cordell's on," Mandy said with glee, her cheeks bulging with popcorn. "So ... tell us again, Payton, what were you wearing when you met him."

Payton sighed. The popcorn hadn't worked.

"For the last time ... I was wearing Trinity's pink dress and my old boots.'

Mandy pulled a face. "I can't believe you weren't wearing those to-die-for shoes we found in the thrift store. They'd be any cowboy's fantasy."

"And every cowgirl's nightmare. They were so uncomfortable."

"What's a blister or two when you're wearing killer heels?"

"Killer heels is right. I don't know how you can even walk, let alone dance, without doing yourself an injury."

Mandy laughed. "All it takes is commitment."

"Well, my only commitment is to my cows, not to impractical sky-high shoes."

"Someday you'll eat those words, Payton Hollis."

"Not in this lifetime."

Mandy's smile widened. "Want to make a bet?"

Payton shook her head at her incorrigible friend and waved to the two Bar V5 wranglers she'd spied sitting in an adjacent bleacher. Charlie Randall would be at the rodeo with her dude ranch guests and would have roped Zack Harris into helping her play tour guide. And going off the rigid line of Zack's broad shoulders he'd much rather be back at the ranch.

Payton shifted on the hard seat and dangled her foot through the gap between her and the person sitting in front. Her butt was numb and she needed to go for another walk but she didn't want to miss seeing Cordell in action. She adjusted the angle of her hat. The sun had shifted in the afternoon sky. Too late, she felt the nudge from Trinity in her ribs and heard her muttered, "Heads up."

Boots clattered on metal as a broad-shouldered, masculine body slid into the spare space beside her. A familiar woody aftershave informed her who her new bench-buddy was. Rhett Dixon.

"Ladies," he drawled as he swept off his Stetson and bowed.

"Hey," they all answered, but it was only toward Payton that Rhett looked. She smiled into his handsome face. He'd been pulling her pigtails since first grade and she'd enjoyed his company until he'd begun his crusade to end her single days.

"Payton, you walked right past me with your popcorn. Didn't you hear me call out?"

"Sorry. The crowd must have been cheering."

"New shirt?"

She gritted her teeth as his blue gaze slid over her chest.

"No, same shirt as when I saw you outside the diner two weeks ago." She kicked his boot. "Rhett, eyes above my collarbones. You know what happened last time you forgot your manners."

"How could I forget? My shiner took a week to go away." His smile turned sheepish. "In my defense, I did have a bit of beer on board that night in Grey's Saloon."

"Well, you don't now, so stop looking me over like I'm a breeding cow."

Beside her, Trinity giggled. "You go, girl," she said in an undertone only Payton could hear.

"Sorry."

"No, you're not. Just don't do it again." But her words didn't contain any bite. Good-looking and blond-haired Rhett was harmless. The first son in three generations of ranchers, he'd led an indulged life. After his mother's recent heart attack, he'd started hanging out with the fast-playing and hard-drinking Taylors. With dimples, a movie-star smile and a host of rodeo wins, he had a parade of buckle-bunnies throwing themselves his way. Her disinterest was a respite. As much as he chased her, she had no doubt deep down he knew he would be safe. She'd never see him as anything but the good friend that he was.

Mandy reached past Trinity to tap Payton's knee. "There he is."

"There who is?" Rhett asked, an edge to his tone.

Trinity waggled her eyebrows. "Payton's new cowboy."

Payton turned to Rhett. "Ignore them. He's not my cowboy. He's just someone boarding at Beargrass Hills while he leases Henry's land."

"How long's he staying?"

The hostile note in Rhett's voice was unwelcome. Despite her clear messages and continued indifference his single-minded pursuit was getting out of hand.

"I'm not sure. He says he doesn't ever stay in any place for long so I've no doubt he'll soon move on."

Rhett didn't answer, all his attention remained focused on the man astride the large black horse waiting for his turn in the tie and rope.

"Well, if his horse's head hung any lower he'd fall asleep."

Payton had seen the speed with which Cordell's horse had whipped his head around to bite him. The black horse was far from sleepy.

"Maybe's he's an old hand and is relaxed," she said.

Rhett lifted a dark-blond brow.

"At least he won't break too early," Trinity piped up, "and earn Cordell a 'cowboy speeding ticket' and ten second time penalty like that last hypo-horse."

Payton smiled. For someone who claimed to go to rodeos for the cowboys Trinity sure knew a lot about tie-down roping.

"Shush, here he goes," Mandy said as Cordell guided his horse into the small square roping area set behind the barrier.

He held a coiled pigging string in his mouth ready for when he'd lassoed the calf and needed to tie three legs together. Her fingers curled into her palms as she waited for the moment when Cordell would nod and the chute operator would release the calf.

Suddenly a brown-and-white calf leapt from the chute and shot toward the middle of the arena. The black hindquarters of Cordell's horse bunched but instead of dashing after the calf, the gelding remained still.

"See," Rhett said with a frown. "What did I tell you? His horse is half asleep."

"No, he isn't. It was a false start. The chute operator

pulled the lever too soon and let the calf out. Cordell hadn't nodded." She didn't meet Rhett's gaze sensing he'd pick up on how closely she watched Cordell. "It happened to me once."

The gate across the arena opened and the calf raced through heading for the company of the other calves in the outside corral.

"Take two," Mandy said as with the arena now clear, Cordell nudged his docile horse a little closer to the barrier.

Cordell nodded to the chute operator and this time when the calf tore from the chute, his horse detonated into action.

Payton barely blinked before Cordell's lariat landed in a neat loop around the calf's neck. He was then off his horse, the calf was on the ground and his legs tied in a half hitchknot. All too soon, Cordell lifted his arms in the air signaling to the field judge to stop the clock.

Cordell then remounted and urged his horse forward to release the tension on the rope anchoring the calf to his saddle. The calf had to stay tied for six seconds. Payton silently counted down from six, her hands unfisted as she reached one. Cordell lifted his hat to the now cheering crowd then smiled and leaned forward to hug his horse's neck.

"I'm no cowgirl," Trinity said in an awed whisper, "but that was fast wasn't it?"

"Yes, dang, it," Rhett said, tone gruff. "That horse sure fooled me. Once he got going, he moved quicker than a firecracker."

Payton nodded, incapable of words. It wasn't Cordell's strength or his expertise with a rope that caused her throat to ache with a strange emotion but the obvious bond between him and his horse.

Rhett turned to look at her and she pulled her hat brim lower to shadow her eyes. Rhett couldn't be privy to her internal disarray. She might not be interested in him but she couldn't have him knowing she was far from indifferent to Cordell.

She was already knee-deep in blue-eyed cowboy trouble.

"I'M SORRY, BUDDY," Cordell said as he lifted the saddle flap to reach the buckle on Mossy's girth. "I shouldn't have pushed you so hard."

Mossy's only answer was a swift flick of his tail.

Cordell tugged at the brass buckle. He shouldn't have let the sight of the blond cowboy sitting too close to Payton short circuit his common-sense. It had nothing to do with him if she had a whole corral full of admirers. But as his adrenalin had surged as the calf had shot from the chute, so had his testosterone. Not that Mossy had needed any encouragement to go faster. His horse always gave his all.

They might have scored a fast roping time but Cordell's restlessness hadn't diminished. He needed to get to the ranch before he saw Payton and to make sure he tied his emotions as firmly as he had the legs of the calf. He lifted the saddle and sweat-dampened saddle cloth from Mossy's back and headed into the trailer.

"Mossy, don't even think about undoing that slip knot," he called out.

He emerged to the sight of Mossy nibbling on the lead rope and Payton standing a body length away watching. For some reason the knowledge she'd left the blond cowboy to find him made him feel far more of a winner than his slick roping time. Careful to not let his feelings show on his face, he went and stood beside her.

She smiled. "So it's okay for you to talk to your horse but it isn't fine for me to talk to my cows?"

He laughed. "You bet."

Her smile grew as Mossy sighed, gave up on the knot and hung his head. "He looks like he's going to sleep. He did that while you were waiting in the roping box."

"He often does. I guess he's seen it all before and doesn't know what all the fuss is about."

"Congratulations on your time. I don't think your roping skills need any polishing. You'll do great tomorrow in the final."

"Thanks, Mossy and I were lucky. And there won't be any final tomorrow."

Surprise creased her brow. "No final?"

"Nope. Mossy and I had fun reliving our rodeo days but we've come to Montana to ranch cattle, not compete. We'll leave the finals to the professionals."

"Fair enough."

He bent to rummage around in the nearby grooming kit for a brush. Mossy didn't need brushing but it was either that or test his theory Payton's soft mouth would taste as sweet as it looked.

Too late he realized Payton had taken a step toward Mossy, her hand outstretched to pat his neck.

"Payton, no." He snagged her waist and spun her into his arms. Mossy's ears flattened, teeth bared and his head swung around. Cordell dragged Payton out of his reach.

Heart pounding, he held her close. Mossy was all show, he wouldn't have bitten Payton, but her fragile bones could have taken a hit from Mossy's hard head.

To his surprise, Payton remained in his hold. The rapid rise and fall of her chest against him let him know that despite her experience with horses she was shocked. Somehow his hand had found the gap between her jeans and her shirt. The bare skin of her satin-smooth back burned his palm. Her hat lay on the ground and he realized the floral scent he'd come to associate with her came from her silken hair. Her neat curves fitted against him like they were made to measure and he forced his arms to relax so he wouldn't draw her that little bit closer.

She leaned back in his hold, gold shimmering in her wide eyes. His gaze dropped to her parted lips as she spoke.

"I … I …"

He dropped his arms from around her as though he'd

been burned by a brand. He was a whisker away from kissing her. Where the hell was his self-control?

He bent to collect her dusty Stetson. "I know, you don't need any help," he said, voice hoarse as he brushed off the felt and pressed the hat into her hands.

"No," she said turning to look at Mossy who again had his head lowered as though asleep. "I was going to say I didn't see that coming." She settled her hat on her head. "Thank you. I did need your help."

"He wouldn't really have taken a chunk out of you but he could have knocked you with that bony head of his."

She rubbed at her forearms as though chilled. "Why does he do it? I saw you hug him in the arena. You obviously have a close bond with him and yet he still tries to bite you too?"

"He's just ornery. He stays at Ethan's ranch when I'm in Denver and Ethan believes it's Mossy's way of saying he misses me."

Her laugh was hollow. "I'd hate to see him if he really took a set against someone."

"Trust me, it isn't a pretty sight. He used to be a buck jumper and he wasn't too keen on particular cowboys."

"That makes sense. I can see him being a buck jumper as well as a crowd favorite. He wouldn't have quit until he had a cowboy off his back."

"He didn't." Cordell rubbed his stiff shoulder. "My first ride, he busted my shoulder."

"And the second?"

"I lasted under three seconds."

Payton laughed again and this time her laughter contained its usual music. "You either are a slow learner or you like living dangerously."

"Both, seeing as I paid top-dollar to buy him to retrain."

"And how did that go?"

"It was a little like the pecking-order issues you had when milking the cow."

"So you landed on your butt, then?"

He grinned. "More than once. But he's the smartest horse I've ever owned and has the biggest heart. I wouldn't swap him for anything."

Cordell picked up the brush he'd dropped and gave Mossy's hindquarters a wide berth as he walked around to his right side. When he brushed Mossy, he now wouldn't have his back to Payton and they could still talk.

Payton stepped closer, keeping an eye on Mossy's head. "So what's he like with other horses, especially if he doesn't like them?"

"And he won't like them. Even though horses are usually herd animals Mossy prefers to be on his own." Cordell paused in his brushing. "Though I think he will like that spirited little mustang of yours."

"Well, she's more than a match for him so he'd better behave himself when he's out at the ranch."

"He will. Speaking of the ranch, is there a key somewhere I can let myself in with? I'll be heading there soon."

Payton bent to select a brush from the grooming kit. Then watching both Mossy's ears as well as his hindquarters she began to brush his withers. "It's fine, I'll be right behind you."

"There's no need to leave on my account, the rodeo is only getting started."

From over in the main arena country music blared and the buzz of the excited crowd signified the barrel racing was over and the bareback riding event would soon follow the intermission.

Payton's only answer was a shrug.

"I've heard there's dancing later and Jake Kohl will sing." Cordell met her gaze over Mossy's back. "What about your friends and the blond cowboy sitting with you in the stands? They'll want you to stay and join in the Saturday night fun?"

He hoped she didn't notice the tension edging his words when he'd mentioned the blond cowboy.

"I've no doubt you've heard about Jake Kohl singing. Any cowgirl with a pulse will be at the dance tonight. As for my friends, they won't expect me to go. I've already said I'm off home. I've a cow and calf to check."

"Payton, seriously, stay. I can do your chores. You can't work all the time. You need to relax and to kick up your heels. Go to the dance. Listen to Jake Kohl sing." Cordell summoned what he hoped passed as a relaxed grin. "After all, I'm pretty sure you have a pulse."

A smile touched her lips. "When I'm not saving my

ranch, I most definitely have a pulse." The laughter in her eyes dimmed and she stepped away from Mossy to return the brush to the grooming kit. "But it's best I go home. Rhett doesn't need any encouragement. Hanging out with him tonight would send the wrong message."

"He's the blond and the one you gave a shiner to?"

She grimaced. "Henry's been talking?"

"He has." Cordell walked around Mossy to also put his brush in the kit.

"It was an accident even though Rhett was out of line. He was sitting next to me in Grey's Saloon and when I stood, he grabbed my butt. My elbow automatically jerked back into his face."

"Ouch. He won't be doing that again."

"I hope not. It's not like him. His family are going through a rough patch and for whatever reason he's gotten himself mixed up with the wrong crowd. I've talked to him and so have his sisters but he won't listen."

"Sisters? Henry said he had a twin?"

"Yes, Kendall. They then have an older sister, Peta."

"That's a name you don't hear often for a girl."

"I know. Her father was so hoping for a boy that when she arrived he changed the spelling of the only name he'd chosen. Even with Rhett being born, Kendall also scored a second-hand boy's name."

"You can bet if Peta and Kendall ever had daughters they'd choose a very girly name."

Payton laughed. "Maybe. I know I would."

"With two sisters and you on his case surely Rhett will come to his senses. And if he doesn't, Mossy and I can sort him out."

"Thanks but I don't need any help handling Rhett. He'll realize soon enough he has zero chance with me."

"How did I know you'd say you didn't need any help?" Cordell said with a grin as he broke eye contact to untie the lead rope and hide his relief she wasn't interested in Rhett.

"I'll see you at the ranch."

He nodded. "Will do."

He watched her go. Mossy rubbed his forehead on the front of his shirt. "I know, Mossy, I like her too." He kept staring at Payton, even though she was now a spot of moving color in the crowd. "And that's exactly why the cattle can't arrive soon enough. We'll be too busy to see her. That's the way it has to be." He looked away from Payton to tug Mossy's black forelock. "We haven't secured Henry's land and come to Marietta to find the answers we need, only to fail now."

Chapter Six

"Mossy, I don't care how big and grouchy you are, you're in huge trouble," Payton said, her hands on her hips. She'd come to check on Gypsy before she did her morning's chores only to find Mossy in with the buckskin. Somehow he'd escaped the corral beside the barn and jumped the wire fence to be with the mare. Payton sighed. Not that Gypsy seemed to mind. Eyes closed, she dozed beside Mossy.

"Does that mean I'm in huge trouble too?" Cordell asked from behind her.

Even before she turned, she knew the only one in trouble was her. The sound of Cordell's slow and deep drawl made her insides curl with warmth. So much for her dawn pep-talk she needed to stay in control if she were to survive living three doors down the hall from him.

"That depends. I heard banging so I assume you've fixed whatever fence Mossy demolished making his great escape."

Head bare, Cordell nodded. "All fixed. Baxter and I will now tackle the far corner of Gypsy's paddock where the fence dips and Mossy would have jumped over. But before we start, I'll get him out of there otherwise you'll never be able to work with her."

"Thanks. Maybe he can go in the next-door paddock. Then at least my corral will remain intact."

"Good idea."

She bent to rub Baxter's neck as he leaned against her legs. She hadn't seen him since breakfast. Cordell hadn't been there a full day and already the kelpie followed him like a shadow. She glanced at Cordell's tanned profile as he opened the gate. Not that she could blame Baxter.

Cordell's dark hair had grown a smidge longer and was tousled as though he'd dragged his hand through the front. His denim jacket, red plaid shirt and jeans had long ago lost their store-bought creases and now fitted like a second skin. Heat fired in her cheeks as she caught herself admiring his denim-clad rear as he walked toward the horses. She tore her gaze away and whistled to Baxter who'd snuck after Cordell. She was getting as bad as Trinity ogling cowboys.

"Stay with me, Baxter Boy. You'll frighten Gypsy, not to mention Mossy will eat you for breakfast." Payton looked to where Mossy had angled his hindquarters toward Cordell and lashed out with a lightning fast hoof. "That's if he doesn't eat Cordell first."

Unfazed, Cordell ran his hand along Mossy's back to his neck, steadying him even as a nervous Gypsy cantered away. Cordell then turned toward the gate with Mossy following.

Payton shook her head. One minute Mossy was set to kick Cordell to California and the next he followed Cordell without a lead rope.

She and Baxter stood a safe distance away as Cordell walked Mossy out of Gypsy's paddock and into his new one.

She then joined Cordell at the gate to watch as Mossy kicked and bucked his way over to where the buckskin mare stood on the other side of the fence.

"Mossy gave me such a look," Payton said, "when he went past that I think if I didn't put him next-door to Gypsy I'd be on the top of his hit list."

Cordell laughed. Without a hat brim shading his face, she had an open view of his expression. Amusement crinkled the corner of his eyes and lightened his irises to a clear blue. Again a memory hovered on the edge of her subconscious. Who did he remind her of? Maybe Rhett, as they both had brilliant blue eyes?

Her gaze lingered. But Cordell's mirth couldn't completely erase the bruise of tiredness that smudged beneath his eyes. She had her suspicions it didn't depend upon where he slept, he always failed to sleep well.

"You know," he said, "Mossy does actually like you. You're the only person, other than Ethan, he's let brush him besides me."

She groaned. "Now you tell me he doesn't like anyone else brushing him."

"Don't worry, I wouldn't have had to tell you, if he'd

didn't like you getting up-close-and-personal with him."

Cordell gazed at Mossy with unconcealed affection. Despite Mossy's contrary nature, Cordell loved his horse. And he'd love a woman with that same unconditional depth and conviction.

She swung away from the man beside her. She had to get away from Cordell as well as her thoughts. She had a ranch to save and a drought to survive. Nowhere on her chore-list did it include falling for a cowboy who didn't plan on hanging around.

"Payton?" He caught up with her, his intent gaze examining her face. "Everything okay?"

"Everything's fine. I've got work to do."

His eyes narrowed. "You're not heading into town for the rodeo finals?"

"Nope. I took half of yesterday off."

"So no chance of you coming for a ride to look at the fences on Henry's land and to show me where all the springs and creeks are located?"

"No, sorry. I've got cattle to check."

"Aren't your cattle on the edge of Henry's land near where my leasehold starts?"

She nodded slowly.

"Then come with me. I was going to take the truck but it's a clear day and perfect for riding."

She glanced at the sky Montana was famous for. Brilliant blue, the cloudless canopy stretched above them like an airbrushed canvas. Cordell was right. It was a beautiful fall day. She felt the tug of the natural beauty that she took for granted. She couldn't remember the last time she rode for pleasure or felt the wind on her cheeks and the sun on her back. Tash, her barrel-racing mare, also deserved a ride longer than the quick jaunt to the main gate.

She arched a brow. "Will Mossy behave himself?"

"Absolutely."

It would be madness to spend more time with Cordell. He already affected her in ways she didn't want to contemplate but after today he'd be busy with cattle work. Besides a ride might be what she needed to clear her head. With Cordell away from the ranch and her self-control refreshed and restored she could then refocus on Beargrass Hills.

She drew a quick breath. "Okay."

THE SPRING IN Tash's hooves and the excited bob of her head as she weaved around the cattle told Payton she'd made the right decision. Cordell rode beside her. Mossy appeared to be on his best behavior. Apart from a small buck when Cordell had settled into the saddle, he hadn't put a hoof wrong.

She smiled as a sleeping calf saw them approach, stood and bolted, tail upright, over to his mother.

Cordell chuckled. "I see what you mean. He doesn't even look like the calf we took to the barn."

"He's such a little glutton but I'm glad he's doing so well." She inclined her head toward a tiny calf who staggered after her mother. "That's the newborn I helped deliver yesterday. She looks so fragile in comparison."

Payton checked the herd for any cows who were on their own and whose udder was swollen. Thankfully there were no further cows that showed signs of calving.

"Fingers crossed," she said to Cordell as he continued to ride beside her, "there's only the three cows to calve as I usually plan to have spring, not fall, calves."

"What happened with those three?"

She pulled Tash to a stop and pointed to where a large black bull emerged out of a gully.

"Trouble, happened."

Cordell stopped and frowned at the bull.

"He has his name for a reason," she continued, "last Christmas he went through four fences to get to the cows and now he's with them again when he shouldn't be."

The bull caught sight of them, stopped and pawed the ground. Cordell flashed her a sharp look.

"I thought you said I was the one living dangerously. Payton, what are you doing with an aggressive bull like him?"

She shrugged. "He was cheap and he has good genetics."

The bull pawed the ground again and his head lowered.

Cordell urged Mossy forward so he stood between her and the bull.

"Payton," he said his voice a low rasp, "turn Tash and go."

She opened her mouth to argue.

"Now," he said in a tone that brooked no argument.

She turned Tash and headed a safe distance away. Hooves pounded behind her and she swung around to see a cloud of dust and the back end of the bull as he retreated to his cows. Cordell and Mossy approached in a slow canter.

As Cordell drew near, his face was as serious as she'd ever seen him. "That bull isn't just trouble he's dangerous. Promise me, you won't take him on yourself."

"Tash and I'll be fine. Besides I usually check the cattle in the truck and he doesn't seem to have a problem –"

"Payton ..." Cordell's word was almost a growl.

"Oh, all right. Joe has already told me I'm not to go near him unless there are two of us and Henry keeps reminding me to call Brock Sheenan to see if he wants him to breed rodeo bulls from."

The tension ebbed from Cordell's rigid torso. "Just as well Joe and Henry have some sense."

"Hey, I have sense. Bucket loads. Need I remind you I'm not the one riding a horse who will chew my arm off the first chance he gets?" Her words lost their heat as she caught the white flash of Cordell's grin. "Okay, funny-boy," she continued with her own smile. "The cattle are checked, so let's go see some fences."

Cordell followed Payton through the various gates that led to the land he'd leased from Henry. He turned for a last look at the bull. The black Angus stood at the fence line, eyes trained on them. Payton might believe she'd be fine handling him, but his gut told him otherwise. He'd ridden enough badass bulls on the rodeo circuit to know the bull might be genetically superior but he was still dangerous.

Fear continued to chill his veins at the thought of Payton possibly being crushed by the bull. He'd already lost a good mate to a brutal rodeo bull. Mossy might appear relaxed but Cordell could tell the veteran horse shared his unease. He could feel his disquiet in every step the horse took.

Cordell rolled his shoulders and focused on the hypnotic swing of Payton's long ponytail across her slender back as she rode in front of him. He should be checking fences and looking for a flat spot to locate portable stockyards not worrying about the self-sufficient cowgirl's welfare. She'd made it more than clear she didn't need his help for anything.

So why then did he feel so compelled to lighten her load and to keep her safe? His attention stemmed from more than his mother having raised him to respect women and to do the right thing. What was it about Payton that undid years of self-restraint? Just when it was crucial that he not feel, his emotions refused to remain banished.

He drew alongside her as she stopped at the top of a rise. Before them snowcapped peaks cast shadows on the lower foothills that rolled into a valley of green. The north wind rippled through the tops of the lush grass that would soon feed Luke's hungry cattle.

"There he is. I can't believe he's still around." Payton shaded her eyes with her hand and gazed into the cloudless sky. A bald eagle floated on a wind current, his white head and tail a dazzling contrast to his dark body.

He stopped watching the eagle to watch Payton instead. He still didn't know what part of his addled brain had asked her to come with him, but he was glad she had. The ride had brought a happy flush to her cheeks and a sparkle to her tired eyes.

He breathed deeply and allowed the crisp air to push aside his tension. He'd never be free but at that moment, riding Mossy in the mountains with Payton, the bonds of his past didn't bind him so tightly.

Payton cast him a contented smile. "I used to love riding here as a child, the hills would be a carpet of yellow, crimson and purples. It's no surprise the nearby Gallatin valley around Bozeman is nicknamed The Valley of the Flowers." She waved an arm to her left. "Over there is a log cabin built by Henry's grandfather. Like my mom, Henry's grandmother loved flowers and with her friends started the local tradition in this part of Paradise Valley of naming ranches after the local wildflowers."

Cordell smiled. "I'd never have guessed of such a tradition, what with Beargrass Hills and Larkspur Ridge Ranch."

"Then there's also Bluebell Falls Ranch, Rose Crown Ranch, Hollyhock Creek Ranch and Fire Weed Ranch." The light in her brown eyes ebbed. "Before my mom got sick we'd come out here when the snow melted and the wildflowers bloomed and think of new ranch names."

"I'm sorry to hear that your mom fell sick."

"Thanks." Payton again stared at the bald eagle. "I don't think she ever got over losing Dad. She hadn't been well for quite a while so when the doctor diagnosed breast cancer in a way, it was a relief to know what was wrong. So I left Montana State, nursed Mom, ran the ranch and finished my liberal studies degree online. The chemotherapy and radiation treatment gave us three more years together and I treasured every day."

Mossy shifted beneath him as the horse sensed his reaction to Payton's quiet words. He loosened his grip on the reins and forced the tension out of his rigid muscles. He knew all about the anguish of losing a beloved mother.

"I'm sure she treasured them too," he said in what he hoped qualified as a casual tone.

"She did. When she was bed-ridden and I'd cut all the flowers in her garden, I'd ride out here and pick the buds from Henry's grandmother's pink rose that still grows at the cabin." Payton's wistful expression contained a host of precious memories. "They'd brighten Mom's room for days."

"So you and Henry have always been close?"

"Yes. My mom and Henry's sister were childhood

friends. They used to ride their horses, meet at the log cabin which is about halfway between the two ranches and swim in the spring-fed creek." She glanced across at him. "So if you need fresh water, head to the cabin and then right past the big pine tree."

He nodded. "You need a spring-fed creek near your barn, either that or a working windmill. It isn't just the bunkhouse that has no water, neither does the barn or the horse troughs."

"I know. Sorry. I should have mentioned there was no trough water. I saw Mossy had some last night in the corral so you must have carted it from the hose near the garden shed. As for the horse troughs, I'll fill them tonight by hand."

"It's fine. I'll do it and maybe I could also take a look at the windmill and get it running before Joe gets back."

Payton gathered Tash's reins. "Thanks but it's fine," she said, voice tight. "Fixing the windmill can wait."

She nudged the mare forward and he lost sight of Payton's face but not the impression his offer to help had ended their ride.

"Okay, I think we've seen enough now," she said, her still clipped tone, confirming his thoughts. "The fences all look good and you know where the water is, let's go home."

CORDELL GAZED DOWN from his position halfway up the

ladder he'd carried from the workshop and rested against the windmill. "If Payton comes out of the house you'll let me know, won't you, Baxter?"

The kelpie wagged his tail.

Payton had said fixing the windmill could wait but it could just be a simple fix that would restore water to the bunkhouse and troughs. The sooner the water supply was returned the sooner Payton could stop carting heavy water buckets to her mustang and the sooner Cordell could move out of the main house. After the morning's ride, he needed to put some physical distance between them. Between worrying about Payton facing off with the bull and grieving for his own mother, he'd lost focus. There was too much at stake for him to allow his feelings to distract him.

Even without reaching the top of the ladder, he could see the problem. The windmill blades tilted at an odd angle. The bolts must have pulled out of the top mount. He'd straighten the mount and then insert new bolts. He'd seen some in a container on a workshop shelf. Easy.

Payton's angry words cut through the silence.

"Cordell, *get down*."

Cordell glanced to his right where the kelpie had been lounging but the dog was nowhere to be seen. So much for Baxter's watch-dog ability. No doubt a rabbit trail had proved more interesting.

"Okay," he said as he took another look at the windmill bolts to see what size he'd need. "I'll grab some new bolts and then fix the mount."

"No, you won't."

He sighed. She sounded wilder than a coyote who'd missed dinner. "Yes, I am. You need to have water."

"Cordell, *please*," her voice broke, "get off the ladder."

He glanced down. Something was going on, more than her being furious at him for helping her. She stood at the bottom of the ladder, her face chalk-white and arms wrapped round her chest.

He scooted down the ladder steps and jumped the last yards to the ground.

He took a step toward her and held out a hand. "What's wrong?"

Mouth pressed into a firm line, she shook her head and swung away, heading for the house.

"Payton, talk to me." Despite the concern deepening his voice he kept his words gentle and calm.

For a moment he thought she wouldn't answer and then she spun around.

Her eyes were dark pools of pain. "Promise me, Cordell, you won't go up the windmill again." She dashed at her cheeks as though suddenly discovering they were wet. "Promise. Me."

"Okay. I give you my word. I won't go up the windmill again." He rubbed a hand across his chin. "What's going on?"

The smooth skin of her throat rippled as she swallowed.

She glanced toward the house and then back at him. Her small chin lifted but when she spoke her words were as unsteady as an earth tremor. "T ... that's how my father died. He f ... fell from the windmill."

Without thought, Cordell covered the ground between them and gathered her into his arms to pull her close. "I'm so sorry."

She stiffened but after a long second relaxed and laid her cheek against his shirt. "I was there." Her words were muffled and he had to strain to hear them. "But I couldn't do anything when his foot slipped ... and then I couldn't save him when he lay on the ground."

Cordell tightened his hold, rested his chin on the top of her silken head and held her until her shaking lessened. Words would prove powerless against her despair. Overhead a black-billed magpie called but Cordell didn't take his attention off the grieving woman who fitted so perfectly in his arms.

The sound of the magpie roused Payton. She eased away a little. Anguish pinched her pale face. For a beat she stared at him and then her pupils dilated as though she realized he still held her. She pulled herself out of his arms and dragging her hair off her face, took two steps backwards.

He forced his arms to remain by his side and not again tug her close. "Many ranches now use solar power; you could do away with the windmill," he said, tone quiet.

She turned toward the ranch house. "I know but replacing it costs money. When it breaks, Joe fixes it but he always does it when I'm not there."

Cordell walked close beside her and made a mental note to make sure she was well away from Beargrass Hills when Joe tackled the windmill. He'd also make sure she would be inside when he removed the ladder and replaced it in the workshop.

"I came to ask what you wanted for lunch," she said without looking at him.

"To tell you the truth, I'm not hungry."

"Me, either."

He glanced toward his truck and spoke before his self-preservation could deliver a mental head-slap. "Perhaps we both need a change of scenery? Shall we go to Marietta? I need some cattle licks and a few other things if anything is open with the rodeo finals on. We could also have a late lunch somewhere?"

She stopped walking. "We went for a ride this morning, I can't now take the afternoon off."

"You won't really be taking it off. I'm sure there are some things you could do in town?"

"I suppose so." Her brow furrowed. "I do have some shoes to offload. I could also see Trinity and Mandy and maybe catch the last of the rodeo action." She hesitated. "Okay. Let's do it."

Chapter Seven

"NICE SHOES," CORDELL commented as Payton slid into the passenger seat of his pickup truck. He'd keep everything light and breezy between them and try and chase the sadness from her eyes.

"Well, if you were a ladies size six, you could have them," she said, tossing the pink sandals at her feet before securing her seat belt. "They are going straight into the charity bin around the side of the thrift store before Mandy can talk me into keeping them."

She sat back in her seat and threw him an exasperated glance tinged with a hint of a smile. "Apparently heels like these are every guy's fantasy, which makes you all very strange in my book."

He grinned and started the truck engine. "They're not my fantasy. I'm more of a boots man."

He glanced at her scuffed boots. And since meeting her, it was boots worn with a very short pink dress.

Payton suddenly leaned forward and the belt pulled tight between her breasts. Scratch the pink dress. Make that boots teamed with fitted jeans and a white and turquoise western shirt. Payton had no idea how gorgeous she was. Even with no heels or boots, she'd be any hot-blooded man's fantasy.

"Look." She pointed to a wooden corral post. "It's a bluebird and probably the last one you'll see until summer."

He looked over to where she indicated and caught the flash of vivid blue before the bird took flight.

"Did you see it?" she asked.

He nodded. "It's such a beautiful bright blue."

"It sure is."

She again sat back in the seat and shot him a smile that this time reached her eyes.

The ball of tension within his chest unraveled. Payton was now doing okay. She had herself back under control.

He sent the truck rattling toward the main gate. Which was more than he could say about himself. Suggesting they travel to Marietta together wasn't exactly his brightest idea. In the close confines of the truck he registered every breath she took and every sweep of her dark lashes as she blinked. Her fresh floral scent filled the cabin and made him yearn for a wildflower-filled summer.

She stretched and dug in her jeans pocket. Again the seat belt pulled tight across her chest. A muscle twitched in his jaw as he concentrated on the road.

"What's your cell number?" she asked. "I'll put it in my phone. Then I can message you if we get separated."

He rattled off his number and focused on the Montana

scenery and not on the cowgirl beside him.

The further they drove from Beargrass Hills the greener and thicker the pastures became. To his left a grove of aspens fringed a meadow, their amber leaves quaking in the sun. Movement caught his eye, and he saw two elk disappear into the trees. He looked in his rear view mirror back toward the stark brown hills of Payton's home. Beargrass Hills had the misfortune to exist in a tiny dry microclimate that had led to its "pocket drought." The rain clouds had to blow Payton's way soon.

Her phone chimed. She pulled it out of her jeans pocket and read the text message. "Mandy wants to know if we would like to go to Grey's Saloon later for beers and burgers?"

"It's up to you, I don't mind. Baxter and the chickens have all been fed and the horses have water so there's no need to rush home."

She pursed her lips. "How about we make it early as I've a busy day tomorrow and your cattle will be arriving?"

"Sounds good."

She typed off a quick message. The phone chimed again. "Now Mandy wants to know if we'll come to the rodeo to see the bronc riding finals?"

"No, you go. I need to buy the cattle licks. I can meet you later at Grey's Saloon."

"Is that okay?"

"Yes." He hoped she'd missed the huskiness in his voice.

The worry in her brown eyes that he mightn't be fine in town by himself had touched him. Usually he was the one making sure everyone else was all right.

"We'll make a quick stop at the charity bin and then maybe you could drop me at the rodeo grounds? I'll text when we get to Grey's Saloon."

"Deal."

TWO HOURS LATER Cordell wished he hadn't made such a deal. After dropping Payton at the rodeo grounds on the outskirts of Marietta his truck felt strangely empty. If he'd thought being away from Payton would settle his emotions, he was wrong. Each time he returned to his truck from running an errand, her floral scent reminded him of the woman who would be cheering on some other cowboy. He only hoped she was having some long-overdue fun.

He'd collected his cattle licks from the Marietta Feed and Supply store that had remained open for any last-minute rodeo needs. He'd also managed to visit Copper Mountain Chocolates. On the floor of his truck rested a paper bag tied with copper ribbon and filled with cowboy-boot-shaped chocolates. He'd purchased the hand-made chocolates on impulse and now wondered what reason he could use to give them to Payton.

While in the mouth-watering store he'd given into his hunger and bought a chocolate-dipped frozen vanilla yoghurt bar. He'd then strolled the main street enjoying the western-themed window displays with their bales of hay, old wagon wheels and rodeo banners featuring the distinctive shape of Copper Mountain. But, even on a sugar high, a cowboy could only do so much window shopping. So he now sat in his truck waiting for Payton to text.

He checked his phone again. Nothing. He tapped his fingers on the steering wheel and stared through the windshield at the rodeo's namesake. Burnished and bright in the late afternoon sun, Copper Mountain stood like a sentinel watching over the town. The snow-shrouded peak appeared identical to the image that had filled his laptop screen when he'd run an internet search on Marietta. And now, just like then, he wished the granite peak could talk. The timeless mountain would be privy to generations of scandals and secrets.

The phone he'd tossed onto the passenger side seat, whooshed. Payton had texted. He scrolled through her message and replied before firing up the truck engine and driving to the corner of First and Main.

Judging from the pickups already parked out the front of Grey's Saloon and the country music blaring over the twin swinging doors, it was already a happening place. His phone whooshed again. He turned and parked across the road near the bank before checking his message.

Payton had seen him drive by and was waiting for him at the entrance of the saloon. He stifled a surge of pleasure and, jaw set, quit his truck. Today had been filled with high emotion, he couldn't let it end the same way. It was time to rein in his feelings.

But as he strode along the sidewalk and Payton smiled as she caught sight of him, the instant lurch in his gut warned him it may be too late.

"Hey," she said, weaving through the rodeo revelers heading inside the saloon. "How was your afternoon?"

"Great. And yours?"

"Good too." Even before she answered, the rich color in her cheeks informed him she'd had an enjoyable time.

Her smile turned shy. "Thanks for suggesting we come into town, it was just what I needed."

"Anytime." He glanced past her, telling himself he was looking for her friends and not the blond cowboy. "Where are Trinity and Mandy?"

"Already inside." Caution eclipsed the smile in her eyes. "Listen Cordell, Rhett drew a bad bull and his ride was over before it started. He was heading straight here and would have a few beers on board by now."

Cordell folded his arms. "Okay. So he's drowning his sorrows. That's understandable." He dipped his head toward the swing doors. "Shall we head in too?"

She reached out and curled her hand around his bare forearm where he'd rolled up the sleeves of his blue western shirt. He failed to suppress a shudder of longing.

"Rhett really is harmless."

"And …"

Cordell didn't need her to complete his sentence to know where this conversation headed.

"And … I can handle him," she said, her fingers still curved around his forearm.

"I have no doubt you can."

She slowly removed her hand. His skin mourned the loss of her warm touch. "So there won't be any problem?"

"Not that I can see."

But as he followed Payton into the saloon and a blond cowboy stopped midway across the room to lock gazes with him, Cordell knew there already was a problem.

Harmless. Yeah right. The flare of possessiveness in Rhett's eyes as he headed straight for Payton tripped every internal alarm Cordell owned.

PAYTON SMILED AS Cordell finished another story about Mossy teaching over-confident cowboys a lesson or two. While Trinity's and Mandy's bursts of uncontrollable laughter filled the small, intimate booth, she examined Cordell in the dim saloon light. Sure his tanned hand might lie relaxed on the table and his other hand grasp a beer, but for the first time she caught a resemblance between him and Mossy. Cordell wasn't a violent man, but there was something about the way he sat that suggested if trouble came his way he would be ready.

Just like Mossy exploding into life in the tie-down roping, Cordell was primed for action. He'd made sure he'd sat on the right side of the booth so he'd have an unhindered view of the saloon. Every so often his eyes would scan the room and linger where the noise and laughter was the loudest. And this was usually where Rhett and his hard-drinking friends played pool. If Payton left the booth for any reason Cordell's gaze remained on her until she was seated again. Instead of making her feel frustrated that he didn't think she could take care of herself, a small part of her appreciated his attention. It felt like a lifetime since she didn't have to shoulder life's burdens on her own.

She stifled a sigh. But there was no point feeling this way. There'd be no happy ending for her like there had been earlier at the rodeo when cowboy, Levi Monroe, had proposed to Selah while being carried away by paramedics on a stretcher.

Cordell took a sip of his beer and as he lowered the bottle, his serious eyes met hers. She felt the jolt to her toes. When Rhett looked at her, she never drowned in the blue of his gaze.

Rhett's laughter sounded in the break between country music songs and she glanced his way. He held up his almost-empty beer glass in a silent toast to her. She shook her head and looked away. She'd made it clear to Cordell she didn't want there to be any problem between him and Rhett. But the way Rhett was drinking it was only a matter of time before he did something reckless. When she'd arrived he'd given her a too tight hug that had lifted her off the ground. Her kick in his shins had then seen him lower her to the floor, his expression apologetic. The whole time she'd felt Cordell's steady presence right behind her.

She faked a yawn. If she didn't want there to be any further issues, they should leave. "Ready to go?" Cordell asked above the din.

"If you are?"

"Yes." He pushed his half-empty beer glass away. It had been his only one for the night. She finished off her iced water. She had a busy day tomorrow too and had only ordered a single beer. She slipped to the end of the booth seat and stood.

Mandy gazed at her with horrified eyes. "No, Payton, you can't go yet. We still have to hear what Mossy did to that arrogant Wyoming cowboy."

Trinity, who was sitting beside Cordell, looped her arm through his, anchoring him in the booth. "We're not letting you leave until you finish your story."

"You guys." Payton laughed. "Cordell can finish his story another day. We have to go."

She turned away to let Cordell extricate himself from Trinity's clutches. Mossy wouldn't be the only one with a repertoire of escape artist skills. Cordell's arm would have been clung onto by many more feminine hands than just her friend's.

By the time she'd reached the wide saloon bar, Cordell would have caught her up and they could leave before any trouble started. But as an arm slipped around her waist and hot beer-breath brushed her cheek, she knew she'd left leaving too late.

"Pay, don't go," Rhett breathed into her ear, "I haven't told you how much I like your shirt."

"You always like my shirt," she said with a smile as she pulled herself from his hold, "and I've got work to do tomorrow."

Rhett grabbed for her waist again. "You always have work to do."

"I know, I'm a busy cowgirl," she said as she again went to pull herself free. This time Rhett didn't let her go.

"Rhett, look at me," she said in her best don't-mess-with-me-voice he'd recognize from first grade. "Let me go."

"Pay, you're so pretty when you're mad." Rhett's mouth lowered. "Just gimme a kiss. I've had such a bad day."

She was about to give him a firm shove, when Rhett's arms dropped from around her. He took a step away, swayed, and expression wary, stared at something over her right shoulder. She swung around. All saloon sounds faded.

Cordell stood still, his arms loose by his side and apparently relaxed. Then she looked into his eyes, eyes that were cold, flat and emotionless. It was as though she was gazing into the face of an old west gunslinger who'd have once frequented the historic saloon. A man who, in that moment, had nothing to lose.

Rhett muttered some words she couldn't catch before she heard the stumble of his boots as he returned to his friends.

"Cordell, I'm fine," she whispered, taking a step toward him. His narrowed gaze remained zeroed in on Rhett. She slipped her hand in his. "Let's go."

She didn't think he'd heard her and then his fingers wrapped around hers.

"Okay," he said, his single word a hoarse rasp.

During the short and chilly walk to the truck, Payton kept her hand linked with Cordell's. If she let go she wasn't sure she could again pull him back from the inner-darkness she'd just glimpsed. If she opened her mouth to speak she wasn't sure she could control the emotions rioting within her chest. She didn't glance sideways as a truck passed and honked its horn or look up at the fairy lights strung between the lampposts like earth-bound stars. She only nodded when Cordell opened the door for her and didn't say a word when he slid into the driver's side seat. But as they left Marietta, she found her voice.

"Pull over."

In the dim light of the truck cabin, Cordell shot her a quick and dark look.

"Now?"

"Yes. Now. And here," she said, indicating where the roadside verge widened and would allow them to pull off a safe distance from the asphalt.

The truck's indicator provided the only sound in the strain as Cordell pulled onto the verge. He killed his lights and then the engine. The moonlight cast a pale glow in the cabin.

She released her seat belt and turned toward him. "What was that all about?"

Cordell's knuckles shone white on the steering wheel before he too unfastened his seat belt. He shifted in his seat to face her.

"Nothing. There wasn't a problem. I didn't touch him."

She'd been around Cordell for long enough to recognize the repressed anger clipping his words. "You didn't have to. I saw your ... face."

"And?"

She frowned. In the moonlight his features were all hard planes, shadows and secrets. "And ... I want to know why you have such a death wish?"

He matched her frown. "Death wish?"

"Yes, this isn't the only time I've seen you take an unnecessary risk. You would have taken on Rhett and every cowboy in that saloon in a heartbeat, not giving a damn about your safety."

He shrugged. "I don't take unnecessary risks. I take calculated risks. There's a difference."

"True, but when it comes to calculated risks we have different definitions. I use emotion to weigh up if a risk is worth taking." She lifted a hand as if to touch him but then laced her fingers together. "And you don't."

His frown deepened. "That's right. I don't. Emotion has no place in decision making."

"Why not? I've seen you with Mossy. I hear the love you have for your brother when you talk about him. You do experience deep emotion. So why do you shut down and go into a place where you don't feel and you don't care, even about yourself?"

His mouth tensed. "Life isn't always a perfect eight-second bull ride, Payton."

She flinched as the raw memories from earlier in the day battered her. "Don't you think I don't know that?"

Apology glittered in the depths of his hooded eyes. He brushed her cheek with tender fingers. "I'm sorry, that was harsh and out of line."

She nodded, wishing the slow and comforting glide of his touch hadn't ended so soon.

"Cordell, your emotions make you human. They make you care that your words were harsh. They anchor you, they protect you. You can't keep on ignoring them, especially when you need them the most."

His expression settled into unreachable lines.

There had to be a way to bypass the emotionless firewall he'd surrounded himself in.

She uncurled her fingers and returned his gesture of comfort by sliding her fingers along the whiskered line of his firm jaw.

"Talk to me," she said, her tone soft as she searched his hewn face for a sign he'd let her in. "Let me help you."

He stiffened but didn't move away from her touch. "So how does that work? You're allowed to help me. First, with prime ribs, then with a coat and cookies and with having a place to stay, and yet I'm not allowed to help you. Period."

She hesitated. The only way Cordell would open up to her was if she gave him a glimpse of the pain darkening her own inner world. Her fingers trembled and she lowered them from his jaw. "It's not that I don't want your help … it's more I can't accept it."

He remained silent as if sensing if he replied she'd lose her nerve and not be able to continue.

She swallowed and then spoke. "I need to stay in control. I couldn't control my father falling, I couldn't control my mother wasting away and I can't control when it will rain, but there are other things I *can* control. If I do everything myself, then I don't feel so powerless or so … hopeless and weak."

Cordell nodded, a muscle working in the taut plane of his cheek. He reached for her left hand, linked his fingers with hers and kissed the sensitive skin on the underside of her wrist.

She shivered at the caress of his lips and the fixed intensity of his eyes.

"Payton," he said, voice husky, "you are the strongest person I know but it's impossible to deal with everything life throws at you on your own. Letting someone share your burdens will only make you stronger, not weaker. There's a reason why all the nearby ranches are named after wildflowers. The pioneers formed a community and together they helped each other carve out a new future."

She gazed at their joined hands. Her fingers looked so fragile and slender against his strength. Was it okay to once again draw upon another's solidity? Before death had stripped the light from her life she'd been better able to accept help. Was he speaking the truth? His considered words were filled with conviction. Could she become stronger by relinquishing control?

"If I consider allowing myself to accept help," she said, her voice an uncertain whisper, "will you allow yourself to feel … and I mean really feel?"

He too stared at their hands and then he slowly nodded.

"Deal."

But the casualness of his tone didn't match the grooves slashed beside his mouth.

This time Payton remained quiet, giving Cordell the space and time to speak.

"But I already do feel," he said, his pained words a rasp in the night-time stillness. "I just … stop myself. Emotions have only ever been a liability. My mother and grandmother spent their lives running from an abusive man. I guess I absorbed their fear. I still can't sleep well, even as an adult."

He paused and her fingers tightened on his.

"Ethan and I were always the new kids in school. I soon learned to blank out my emotions and to use my fists to protect us. In my teens I started testing myself by taking risks to make sure I wouldn't feel and I guess I haven't stopped. One of the reasons I took Mossy on was because I can never relax around him."

"Well, you got that one right."

The corners of Cordell's mouth briefly curved.

"You are a good and decent person," she continued, "and it is your emotions that make you this way. You can't keep shutting them out and taking dangerous risks because ..." Her voice cracked as the image of him halfway up the windmill replayed in her mind. She placed her palm against his face. "One day your luck might run out."

With her left hand still entwined with his, it was as though by touching his lean cheek with her right hand she'd completed an electric circuit. A current of awareness flowed through her, quickening her breathing. As Cordell's eyes darkened to near black, she knew he'd felt it too.

"Payton." His gaze dropped to her mouth and her name was more a groan than a word.

She leaned forward. It didn't matter if Cordell would soon be gone. Even without his mouth covering hers, she was lost. There was no doubt she was a cowgirl with a pulse. A pulse that only beat for Cordell.

He closed the small space between them. His warm breath washed over her mouth. Her lips parted.

White light speared through the misted truck windows. "Get a room," a man's voice shouted before a car horn wailed.

The moment shattered like her mother's floral bone china on the slate kitchen floor.

She jerked back, pulling her left hand free and her other hand away from Cordell's face. What had she done?

She'd lost control and let down her defences. She'd wanted to gain access into Cordell's world to ease the pain that held him and his emotions hostage. She wasn't supposed to then hand him the password to her soul.

She sat back in her seat and closed her eyes to break the connection with the man beside her who watched her closely, his eyes bleak and his mouth compressed. She hadn't only rendered herself vulnerable, she'd also jumped to the front of the Marietta gossip queue.

Everyone had seen her leave Grey's Saloon hand-in-hand with Cordell. Now his pickup, with its white and green Colorado mountain plates, was seen stationary with steamy windows. They may as well have been caught necking at the teenage make-out spot up at the lookout at Bobcat Hill.

She rubbed her forehead. Dealing with a remorseful and hung-over Rhett tomorrow would be the least of her worries. Trinity and Mandy were going to have a field day.

Chapter Eight

THE FRONT DOOR squeaked as it opened and Payton's heart did a funny little leap. Cordell was back. He'd left the ranch house before she'd woken and for some reason until she saw him her day didn't seem to be able to start. Ever since the cattle trucks had arrived and the black Angus were unloaded she'd hardly seen him. It was as though after their emotion-charged talk and near kiss, they'd made the mutual decision to keep out of each other's way. Every so often their eyes would meet and lock, but then one of them would look away and the no-go safety zone between them be reestablished.

Payton's phone had run red-hot after their ill-fated roadside stop. Town gossip queen, Carol Bingley, had been the first to call. Now, five days later, the town's attention had shifted to another juicy gossip item. According to Mandy, who heard all the up-to-date news working in the local hair salon, some stock had gone missing from Hollyhock Creek Ranch and three pairs of cowboy boot tracks had been found.

Payton tucked a loose strand of hair behind her ear and brushed the dust off her worn jeans. At least with Cordell spending so much time with the Texan cows any would-be cattle rustlers wouldn't have a hope of nabbing them. Boots sounded on the hallway floorboards and she busied herself rinsing the coffee pot. She didn't want Cordell to think she'd been waiting for him.

"Payton?" A man's voice called out. She stifled a pang of disappointment. The voice and footsteps didn't belong to Cordell.

"Hi, Henry," she said, "I'm in the kitchen."

She placed the coffee pot in the draining rack with the mug Cordell had used and washed at whatever hour he'd woken. She dried her hands on the dishcloth hanging from the cupboard handle.

As the old rancher entered the kitchen, she greeted him with a cheery smile.

"You're in time for coffee, cookies and chocolate."

Henry's grey eyes smiled. "As usual my timing is perfect."

"It sure is."

Henry sank into the wooden chair at the kitchen table and she assessed his expression. She'd never seen him look so shocked and so old as when he'd witnessed the horse knock over the pram at the rodeo. But today his face was its normal tanned hue.

"So how's that mustang coming along?"

"Good," she said as she placed a plate of oatmeal raisin cookies in front of him. "You won't believe it but that cranky horse of Cordell's has really calmed her down."

She took Sage's hand-made chocolates from the fridge and untied the bag's copper ribbon.

"Stranger things have happened." Henry looked at the chocolates. "Someone's been shopping?"

"Cordell."

"Well, I'll say one thing, he hasn't wasted any time getting to know Marietta if he's already found Sage's store."

"I know," Payton said, as she placed the sweet-smelling cowboy-boot chocolates in a glass bowl. As she set the bowl beside the plate of cookies Henry traced a pattern on the smooth table surface with his blunt finger.

"Has he been asking questions when he's been making himself at home in town?"

"No, I don't think so. He's only ever asked me about Rhett's sisters." She looked up from where she poured two mugs of coffee. "Why?"

"No reason. Just curious. He just strikes me as a man who likes to know what's going on."

"He does." She carried the coffees to the table and then sat at the table too. "You know, I can't help but think he reminds me of someone but I can't for the life of me work out who."

Henry took a second to answer. "Cowboys nowadays all look the same, not like back in my time. Take Rhett, since he started hanging out with those Taylor boys, he's grown his hair long and wears jeans at least a size too small like every other fancy cowboy." Henry drew his coffee toward him. "You still doing okay for hay?"

Payton didn't miss the quick change of subject. "Yes. But I thought you were sending a few bales over for Gypsy, not a whole truck."

Henry's lips twitched. "There must have been a mistake with the order."

She sent him a mock frown. "I bet there was."

"You'll be right now for hay until it rains. Which might be sooner than you think. The weather channel says a storm will be coming through in the next twenty-four hours."

"I sure hope so. None of the predicted storms ever seem to come my way." She selected a cookie to hide the desperation her face would reveal. "I've forgotten what rain looks like."

"It'll rain. Don't you worry about that. And the way my hip aches, it's going to be some storm."

He stared at the single coffee mug in the draining rack. "When are Joe and Maria back?"

"Three days and I'm counting. I might love baking cookies but I sure struggle preparing a proper meal."

"I bet they're enjoying seeing their new little granddaughter?"

"They would be." She took a sip of coffee. It was a cruel world that had never allowed Henry to have children.

"I hear you and Cordell caused quite a stir Sunday night."

"I'm sure you did. Was that before or after Grey's Saloon? And is that the version where I did, or didn't, have my shirt on when I gave him a lap dance in his truck?"

Henry chuckled. "The version where you and Cordell talked."

"Oh. Who told you that? I didn't think there was a true version out there?"

"Cordell. He called. He didn't want me to think he wasn't minding his manners."

She laughed. "That's right, you mentioned Rhett's shiner to him. I might have known you'd told him to behave himself. You'll be glad to know I won't ever have to give Cordell a black eye. His manners are flawless and, like me, he's only interested in his cows."

She expected Henry to laugh too but instead his shrewd gaze flickered over her face.

She was never so glad to hear Baxter bark. She pushed back her chair to collect another coffee mug. "Speaking of Cordell, he and Baxter are back."

Boots sounded and then the soft fall of socked feet after Cordell removed his boots in the mudroom. He walked through the doorway, his shirt and jeans covered in dried mud.

He shook Henry's hand and then smiled across at her as she poured him a coffee. "Hey, Payton."

"Hey." She only hoped Henry would associate the flare of warm color in her cheeks with drinking her too-hot coffee.

Cordell sat at the table, careful not to transfer the dirt from his clothes onto the floor. She gave him his coffee and then returned to her seat before his easy grin of thanks weakened her sensible knees.

"Henry, when were those cattle troughs of yours last cleaned?" Cordell asked as he reached for a chocolate with a clean hand. He must have made a stop at the garden tap before coming inside.

"Good question." He dipped his head toward Cordell's shirt that was more dust-brown than blue. "I take it they're clean now?"

"As a whistle. Which is more than I can say about Baxter and me."

"I thought one of your cattle might have looked poorly yesterday but he seems to have picked up today."

Cordell kinked a brow. "You either have super-human vision, Henry, or that was a pair of binoculars I saw the light shining on the other day."

The two men exchanged broad smiles.

Payton smiled too, her heart full. She'd been right in thinking the afternoon she'd met Cordell that he and Henry might get on. Despite their age, the steadiness of their gazes and their innate decency had suggested to her they would respect each other and could become friends.

Henry's rare laughter boomed as Cordell cracked a joke.

She wrapped her fingers around the warm sides of her mug to banish her growing chill. The small kitchen might be filled with companionship and fun this morning but it was only a matter of days before Cordell would move into the bunkhouse and then out of her life for good.

She stood, coffee unfinished. She couldn't stay in the cozy kitchen any longer. She had to get back to work and the things she could control.

"I'll leave you two to enjoy the cookies and chocolates, I've got chores that won't do themselves."

HALF-AN-HOUR LATER, CHEST tight and breaths ragged, she tore into the kitchen. Henry's pickup was gone from out the front of the ranch house and from the sound of running water, Cordell was taking a shower.

She sped along the hallway and hammered on the guest bathroom door.

"Cordell."

The shower stopped and the door flew open even as Cordell secured a low-slung white towel around his lean hips.

All air quit her lungs.

High heels and boots weren't her fantasy, just a water-slicked Cordell smelling of soap and sunshine.

Distracted by a rivulet that seemed to be taking its sweet time sliding over his hard-packed abs, for a split-second she forgot what the emergency was.

"Payton?"

Cordell's hoarse, almost desperate, tone brought her gaze back to his face.

"Mossy's gone."

The strain tensing his mouth eased a notch. "It's fine. He'd have performed another Houdini act."

Cordell looked past her as if wanting her to step away from the door to let him pass.

"No." She grabbed at his arm that held his towel in place. Beneath her fingertips his hot skin seared and his muscles grew rigid. "The gate's wide open. There's boot tracks and hoof marks; however he left, Mossy didn't go willingly."

Anger flashed through the blue of Cordell's eyes. But as quickly as the emotion appeared it disappeared. His gaze turned icy and impassive. But as she let go of his arm and she stepped aside, he dropped a gentle kiss on her forehead.

"He'll be okay, Pay. I'll throw on some clothes and we can go search for him."

She followed Cordell down the hallway. Despite her fears she might know who had taken Mossy, her hormones appreciated their near-naked and tanned cowboy view before Cordell shut his bedroom door.

"It couldn't have been Rhett," she said through the wood, chewing on the side of a nail.

Silence.

"He wouldn't do such a thing."

The door opened. Cordell emerged, face expressionless. His fingers buttoned his emerald-green shirt but not before she'd seen the beads of water glistening on his collarbones. She folded her arms to stop herself from sliding her palms inside his shirt and over his golden skin to brush them away.

"No comment," Cordell said, jaw set as he strode along the hallway to the mudroom. "You'd better call the hospital."

"It wasn't him," she said but her words contained no conviction. There were three boot tracks found at Hollyhock Creek Ranch where the cows were taken. Rhett had been hanging out with three lots of cowboy trouble in the form of the Taylor boys.

"He'll be there if he tries to ride him," Cordell said as he stopped beside the coat rack and pulled on his boots.

Payton reached for her own boots. "But he's a rodeo rider, he'll be fine riding any horse."

"Not Mossy." Cordell's serious eyes met hers. "Call the hospital. If he's not there, then we'll need to look for Rhett as well as Mossy."

As she headed into the kitchen to use the landline, Henry called from outside.

"Hello, the house. I think you might be missing a certain black horse that nearly took my arm off."

Mossy.

She rushed to the window to see Mossy walking behind

Henry, his head hanging low as if he were a placid, bombproof child's pony. Her brows lifted. Mossy might have snapped at Henry but his resistance must have been a token one. The lead rope Henry held, and the head collar Mossy wore, were the ones Gypsy had used when she'd arrived. Payton had returned them to Henry and they would have still been in his truck.

Cordell strode out from the front porch and she opened the kitchen window to hear their conversation.

Cordell shook Henry's hand and then stood still as Mossy rubbed his head against his green shirt.

"I didn't think he'd get too far even though he's probably been out since last night," Cordell said, running his hand down the horse's legs, checking him for injuries.

"He got far enough. He was running along the fence line stirring up Payton's temperamental bull. Just as well I'd decided to head into Marietta otherwise I'm sure Trouble would have broken through the fence to get to him."

She turned away from the window to reach for the phone. Now that Mossy was accounted for she needed to check where Rhett was. Surely what Cordell said couldn't be true? Rhett wouldn't be in hospital. Mossy had had human help to escape but her childhood friend wouldn't be crazy enough to ride him, even if egged on.

She dialed the number for the Dixons' Bluebell Falls Ranch. Kendall's smooth voice sounded at the other end. "Kendall Dixon speaking."

Except this time her usual serene tone was tense and distracted.

"Hi Kendall, it's Payton, I'm after Rhett."

"Hi, Pay, I'm so glad you called. Rhett's been in Marietta hospital since the early hours of the morning. Somehow he's broken some ribs and injured his knee. He didn't come home last night, which is normal these days, so who knows what he's been doing."

Payton's fingers tightened around the phone receiver. She knew. "Whatever he was doing, a stay in hospital will make sure he won't be doing it again. Give my love to your mom and tell her I'll check on him."

"Thanks. Peta and Dad have gone in, I'm giving Mom her lunch and then I'll go too."

"Okay. I'll see you there."

She slowly replaced the handset. Wait till she saw Rhett. His father and sisters wouldn't chew him out, but she would. His injuries would soon be the least of his worries. His days of hanging out with the Taylors were over. His sick mother didn't need any more worry.

BOTH MOSSY AND Cordell turned as Payton's truck tires spun on the gravel as she left for Marietta.

"I hope you went easy with him, Mossy, because something tells me Payton's about to tear strips off Rhett."

Mossy's head dipped lower and he closed his eyes as

Cordell brushed the stiff sweat from his black coat.

His anger at Mossy possibly being hurt had flared like a struck match and then faded as he'd doused all emotion. But now embers continued to smolder. It wasn't Rhett who needed to be taken to task but the three cowboys he hung around with. From the similarity of their thin faces, he'd quickly identified them as brothers. He'd also noted how they'd plied Rhett with alcohol. When he next saw Rhett, after he'd let him know what a fool he'd been, he'd ask where the brothers could be found. His gut told him they weren't going anywhere in a hurry. But they would when he'd finished with them. No-one messed with his horse.

Mossy sighed as Cordell found his sweet spot below his withers.

He glanced in the direction Payton had driven. The other night in his truck he'd been seconds away from finding Payton's own sweet spot. And even now the thought of kissing her made the blood pound through his veins. There was a reason why every shower he'd had since then had been a cold one. Including the one this morning when she'd bashed on the door.

Even knowing there was a crisis, it had taken all of his will-power to not haul her against him and feel the slide of her hands over his wet body. As it was her wide eyes had travelled over his bare chest with the intensity of a physical touch. A small towel had provided scant protection from what she did to him.

He paused in brushing Mossy's flank. He had to get himself under control. He'd meant what he said to Henry, Payton was off limits. He couldn't start something with her only to then leave. She deserved someone far better.

As for why he and Mossy had really come to Marietta, the day was drawing near when his asking of careful questions had to end. And then there'd be only one thing left to do. To act.

The gathering breeze washed across his face. He looked at the sky that was no longer a calm, pristine blue. Clouds, swollen and heavy, hung over the high-country.

A storm would soon roll in.

PAYTON BREATHED A sigh of relief when she saw Rhett's hospital room free from visitors. She'd stopped to chat to a worried Peta and her taciturn father in the parking lot. Kendall was on her way in from the ranch, so Payton had a small window in which to ensure Rhett's rabble-rousing days with the Taylors ended.

She knocked quietly on his door and as Rhett opened his eyes she went in.

"Hey, cowboy," she said as she kissed his whiskered cheek and put the bag of salted caramels she'd stopped to pick up from Copper Mountain Chocolates on the nightstand.

"Hey," he croaked.

She pulled a chair toward the bed and took his hand.

As his guilty gaze met hers she knew, despite his pain, he was lucid enough for the conversation they had to have.

"What were you thinking?" she asked, without a smile.

He didn't pretend to not know what she was talking about.

"I'm sorry. It seemed like a good idea at the time."

"A good idea after drinking all night with the Taylors?"

"They said it would teach Cordell for messing with my girl."

She squeezed his fingers. "What am I going to do with you? You know I'm not your girl."

He sighed. "I do. Now."

"You do?"

"Yes, after seeing you with Cordell at Grey's."

She frowned. "I'm not Cordell's girl either. Those stories about what happened after we left Grey's are rumors. All we did was talk."

"I know. But you are his girl. I've never seen you look at anyone like you look at him."

"Rhett, it doesn't mean anything. You know I only have time for my ranch. Besides, he'll be gone soon."

"Will he? I saw the way he looked at you too." This time Rhett squeezed her hand. "You're special, Pay. Really special. I want you to be happy, even if it's not me putting the smile on your pretty face. Do you love him?"

She stayed silent. The ache in her chest answered for her.

She hadn't even admitted such a truth to herself, but yes, she loved Cordell. Her easy-smiling and gorgeous cowboy had brought light and laughter into her life and pushed aside the loneliness she'd always hidden. From the start, he'd surprised and intrigued her, but most of all he'd understood her.

She nodded slowly.

"Well then, if Cordell can ride that devil of a horse he's the right man for you."

She gave a small grin. "I'm not sure I like being compared to Mossy let alone to the devil?"

"I'm saying nothing that you don't already know. You need a strong man, Pay, you wouldn't be happy with a lap dog. And this cowboy … as much as I hate to say it, he's the right person for you."

Her smile faded at the sadness in his voice. "Rhett, you'll find the right person too. There's a girl out there waiting for your paths to cross."

"I won't be walking for a while, let alone crossing any paths."

"Yes, you will and you will cross the right girl's path. You have to stop being someone that you're not. I know it's hard since your mom had her heart attack. But getting drunk every night and hanging out with the Taylors isn't going to make you feel any better or numb your fear that you will lose her." Her thumb brushed his hand. "You are special too. Be true to yourself and the rest will follow."

Rhett's nod and the gravity of his eyes confirmed he'd

heeded her words. "Any other things, Miss Bossy Beargrass."

She heard light footsteps in the hospital corridor. Kendall had arrived. Payton stood, still holding onto Rhett's hand. Her work here was done if he was calling her by the pet name he'd favored while they were growing up.

"Yes,' she said with a gentle smile, "get a haircut."

Chapter Nine

THE SOUND OF drumming on the ranch house roof merged with the hoof beats pounding through his dreams. Cordell's eyes snapped open. Mossy. When he registered he was lying on his stomach in a double bed that featured a headboard covered in a white and pink floral fabric he knew where he was. Three doors down from Payton in the main house of Beargrass Hills Ranch. He also knew Mossy was safe.

His mental fog cleared a little more and he realized the storm had arrived and with it rain. Relief swept through him. Payton would be happy. He flipped onto his bare back and allowed the tension to drain from his arms and legs. The mustang mare would be used to being outside in the elements and so too was Mossy. In each horse's paddock there was also a sheltering grove of pines. Likewise the Texan cattle would also have plenty of opportunities for shelter with the abundance of trees and draws.

What time was it? He turned his head to check the luminous dials of the bedside alarm clock and groaned. It was two in the morning. He'd only slept for an hour. He folded his arms behind his head and stared at the pale ceiling as he'd done each night now for almost a week.

Usually he couldn't sleep because of his ingrained need to know where he was and to be ready for trouble. But now his poor sleep had more to do with a Montana cowgirl than with habit.

When Payton had returned from seeing Rhett it'd been late. Cordell had done the chores and after raiding the refrigerator and larder had fashioned some passable sloppy joes. She'd been unusually quiet during dinner. He was also sure she'd blushed when he'd caught her looking at him, an indefinable expression clouding her eyes. She'd then pleaded tiredness and headed to bed early. At least when she woke in the morning, if the storm hadn't already woken her, it would be to a wet world.

Above the wind and the rain a dog barked. Had he also heard laughter? He pushed himself into a sitting position and listened. Thunder rumbled but not before he'd caught the unmistakable sound of a woman laughing.

He threw off the bed covers. What was Payton doing outside? All hell would soon break loose. The storm was only beginning. He grabbed a black T-shirt and pulled on a pair of grey sweatpants. Then, bare footed, he padded along the cold hallway floorboards, through the open front door and out onto the lighted porch. Rain streamed from the full gutters and fell in thick ropes of water. It was as though

Mother Nature delivered a year's worth of rain in a single deluge.

The soft glow of the porch light illuminated the girl and the dog dancing in the rain. Dressed in a soaked pink tank top and clinging pajama shorts she kicked at the puddles. Baxter, his liver-red coat dark with water, jumped around her feet. Unaware of Cordell's presence, she stopped. Arms outstretched, she turned her face to the sky, smiled and closed her eyes.

Something in his chest tightened and then tore.

He'd never seen anyone more beautiful. He'd never met anyone who affected him so much. She'd gazed at him through her open truck window and tilted her chin, daring him to judge her as helpless, and had sent his world into a spin. And it hadn't yet stopped spinning. She made him feel. Need, protectiveness, contentment.

Love.

He couldn't deny it any more. He loved the breathtaking, brave and free-spirited cowgirl before him.

His hands fisted by his side. But he could no more tell her how he felt than he could hurt her. He wasn't programmed to stay around. He should return inside. It wasn't his right to share in her happiness. He went to turn away when lightning zigzagged across the jet-black sky. Payton didn't flinch or open her eyes as rain continued to fall on her upturned face. He hesitated. He also couldn't leave her out here with the center of the storm soon to hit.

He stepped to the edge of the porch and called her name into the wind. Her arms lowered and she swung around.

He motioned at her to join him on the porch. With Baxter at her side, she splashed her way over, dripped water over his feet and took hold of his hand.

"Come on, who says I don't ever have any fun?"

Her eyes shone with such golden life, her smile contained such uninhibited joy, all he could do was nod and follow. Getting wet was a small price to pay for stealing a few brief minutes with her in a swirling and surreal world. When the clouds parted and the rain stopped, reality would return. He'd have a promise to keep and a city existence to return to.

Within seconds, he was saturated. Water seeped through his cotton T-shirt and ran down the back of his neck. But as cold as the water was, the feel of her fingers entwined with his, heated his blood. Thunder boomed followed by an almost instantaneous lightning flash. The storm was almost directly overhead. Knowing the wind would steal his words, he tugged her toward the porch. Again, she shook her head. Baxter, his tail between his legs, fled to the safety of his dry kennel.

Thunder again roared. Cordell snagged Payton's slender waist and slung her over his shoulder. He reached the porch just before a jagged bolt splintered the sky.

Chest heaving, he firmed his hold on the back of her knees as he readied himself to return her to the ground. Cool air brushed his lower back and stomach. Payton must have gripped the bottom of his T-shirt to balance herself and had pulled it midway up his torso. He carefully took her weight and lowered her to the porch floorboards. But as he did so her full breasts pressed against his chest and her bare skin slid against his. He bit back a groan. The wet friction between the cotton of his shirt and her tank top had caused her own shirt hem to ride upward. There was now nothing between their naked midriffs but the wet lick of water.

His hands moved to her waist to steady her as her feet touched the ground. Beneath the pads of his fingers, he could feel the jut of her hips and the ripple of goosebumps over her soft skin. He fought for control. She'd be mad at being slung over his shoulder like a sack of grain. It would be okay. She'd tell him off and step away before he did something they'd both regret.

She didn't move.

The soundtrack of the storm's fury dulled to a whisper.

Every breath she took pushed her chest closer to his. Every breath he took threatened to shatter his self-control. When had she laced her hands around his neck? Another three seconds, and he'd be finishing what they'd started in his parked truck.

He didn't even make it to two.

His mouth covered hers. She tasted of rain and sweetness. Smelt of summer and mountain wildflowers. As she stood on tip-toe to match his hunger, the sky could have caved in over him and he wouldn't have cared.

As much as she took, he gave. And as much as he asked for, she granted.

Her hands unclasped from behind his neck and slid over his water-slicked abs and under his T-shirt. He shuddered, knowing he was exposed but powerless to hide how she moved him and what she made him feel.

"Payton," he groaned as they came up for air. "I can't hurt you. I can't stay."

"I know," she said, before again fusing her mouth with his.

His hands found the neat curve of her butt and pulled her even closer. This time she was the one who spoke as they drew apart to breathe.

"Please, tell me you're feeling."

"Oh, I'm feeling all right," he growled as he plundered the delicate line of her soft throat.

"Good, because if you're feeling, as per our talk the other night, that means I need to learn to accept help." He'd never seen her eyes so luminous or heard her voice so breathless. She jumped and he caught her as she wrapped her slim legs around his waist. "And I think I'll start by you helping me get out of these wet clothes."

FOR THE SECOND time, Cordell awoke to the sound of rain on the ranch house roof. But this time the raindrops were intermittent. This time daylight peeked through the pink floral drapes. He smiled. This time he had a naked Payton in his bed.

"What are you smiling at, cowboy?" Payton said, from beside him, her words husky with sleep.

He tucked her closer against his side and kissed the top of her tousled head.

"Nothing."

The hand that rested on his chest slowly slid down to the sensitive skin of his stomach. His breath hissed.

"Nothing, huh?"

"Nothing." His own fingers trailed along the curve of her hip. "Well, I guess it has rained."

"It has. Finally. Any other reason?"

"Well … it's wet outside so I can have a lie-in."

Her hand travelled lower.

"Any other reason?"

He caught her fingers and lifted them to his lips. He needed a second to make sure when he spoke he had his emotions firmly in check.

"And I slept well because you were with me."

Her smile shone sunrise bright. "Correct answer, cowboy."

She sat, pulling the sheet with her to cover her chest. But he already knew the perfection that now lay hidden beneath the bed sheet. His hands and mouth had memorized every satin dip, curve and hollow.

"Seriously?" he said with a frown. "You're getting out of

bed?"

"Yes, you know a cowgirl's work is never done."

She pressed a lingering kiss to his lips. "I'll check the horses and I also want to check my calves. They haven't ever seen rain and those gullies will be streaming with water. Now shut your eyes."

He did as she asked.

She kissed his closed lids. Her silken hair brushed his chest.

"Get some more sleep because when I return you'll have things to smile about. This cowgirl might have work to do, but she also knows how to play."

AN HOUR LATER, Payton had more things on her mind than showing Cordell her playful side. She pressed her foot on the gas pedal but instead of moving forward the truck remained stationary. Dammit.

She'd driven through the pasture conscious of the truck wheels becoming bogged but she'd thought this flat patch of dirt would have provided good traction. But as her tires spun there was no doubt she'd misjudged the water-logged ground. She blew out a frustrated breath and gazed through the mud-splattered windshield to where the cows and the two calves watched her.

She pressed her foot on the gas again. The truck slid forward a body length; she changed gears to reverse and to rock the car out of the grooves cut in the wet earth. But the wheels couldn't get a proper grip. Small clods of mud kicked up by the churning tires, showered the truck cabin roof. She eased her foot off the gas pedal and the revving of the truck's engine quietened.

A black object moved in her peripheral vision and she looked out the side window. Trouble had left the herd and walked closer. Even with the distance between them, she could see the latent power in the thick slope of his shoulders and his broad forehead. She really should give Brock Sheenan a call and see if he wanted the bull. Cordell was right, he wasn't the safest and most predictable creature to have around. She'd tolerated his bad temper knowing his elite genetics would flow through to his offspring. But the longer he stayed, the more he lived up to his name.

She'd try one more time to go forward and if that didn't work, she'd go to Plan B. Walk home and get the tractor. The phone in her jeans pocket vibrated. She pushed aside the denim jacket she wore and took out the phone. Henry's name illuminated the screen.

"Hi, Henry."

"Hi, Payton. Cordell with you?"

She was glad Henry couldn't see her face because the heat that flooded into her cheeks at the mention of Cordell's name would have been a dead giveaway of the night they'd shared. Her lips curved. A tender and sleepless night that even now made her breath catch.

"No, he's ... at the ranch."

"Thought so. Otherwise, he'd be out pushing by now."

"Henry, where are you?" She looked around but all she saw was that the bull had moved closer. "How do you know I'm bogged?"

Henry chuckled. "My superhuman vision."

"Ah, your binoculars."

She opened her window and waved in the direction of Larkspur Ridge Ranch where it nestled high against the mountains.

"See that?"

"Sure did. Now can you get out or do you want me to come and give you a tow?"

"No, thanks. You stay inside where it's warm."

"You've been there for a while, you know."

She sighed. "I know."

"It's a fair walk home for the tractor and there's more rain coming."

She glanced at the ominous gun-metal grey clouds that hung low overhead. "I know that too."

"It's either have me come down or I can call Cordell and get him to drive the tractor to you."

She thought of the peacefulness of Cordell's expression as she watched him sleep and the tell-tale dark circles that appeared a permanent fixture beneath his eyes when he was awake. She didn't want to interrupt his lie-in. "No. If it really is okay, maybe you could come down?"

"I'm already in my truck."

"Henry!"

"See you soon."

She killed the pickup's engine and pulled her jacket closer to her chest. The bull now worried her. He'd stood closer to the immobile truck than he ever had before and had turned side on as though trying to intimidate her with his size. She'd never stopped around the cattle before, perhaps it was only moving trucks he kept away from? She honked her horn but he didn't move. As plump raindrops fell on the truck cabin she turned the ignition key so she could use her windshield wipers. She wanted to know where Trouble was at all times.

It wasn't long before she heard the diesel chug of Henry's truck. Behind her it was still bare dirt but in front of her there was a rise with both good vegetation and drainage that would provide enough grip for Henry's tires. He'd have to drive around the bogged truck and position himself so a chain could be hooked between the two vehicles. He would then drive forward and pull the stuck pickup free. The trouble was the path from the gate to the front of her truck was where the now head-shaking bull stood.

But as Henry slowly drove toward the bull, all he did was flick his tail, turn and amble away. She released her held breath. Trouble wasn't going to prove a problem. Henry waved as he drove past and pulled to a stop. She saw him unfasten his seat belt and turn to judge the distance between them before he reversed.

Too late she saw a flash of black as the bull spun around. Head lowered and shoulders hunched he powered toward the driver's side of Henry's truck.

She honked her horn and called out but the impact of the solid bull hitting the truck door drowned out all other sound.

Heart in her throat, she threw open her passenger door and slid through the mud to the front of her truck. She crouched and when the bull retraced his steps, she ran low to the ground to the passenger side of Henry's car. She slipped into the truck, her knees quaking. Henry sat slumped in his seat, blood on his forehead. She needed to get his truck moved outside the bull's flight zone so he'd cease seeing them as a threat. Then she needed to get help.

The bull pawed the muddy ground, readying for another assault. The truck's engine continued to idle. She couldn't move Henry but as the vehicle was an automatic, if she could put the column-shift into drive, gravity would propel the truck forward. She fiddled with the column-shift and the car rolled, quickly gathering momentum. She leaned over and with one hand turned the steering wheel and with the other grabbed and then secured Henry's seat belt.

This time when the bull hit, he made contact with the tailgate. Payton lurched forward. She steadied herself and took advantage of the truck's momentum down the slight slope. She prayed her quick assessment of a gap within a nearby cluster of fir trees would be correct. As the truck glided between two trunks and the vehicle slowed to a stop on the level ground, she put the column-shift into park.

At least now the low branches would protect the truck's sides and leave only the front and the back vulnerable. The sturdy fallen branch out her window would then give her a weapon should they now not be far enough away. She could only hope Trouble would think the threat to himself and his herd had passed and he would turn away.

Shoulders shaking, she turned to see where the Angus bull was. He stood at the top of the rise. Blood dripped from his nose and as he shook his head, the action one of pain and not aggression. For the moment, they were safe.

She whipped out her phone and dialed 911. She then called Cordell. As he picked up, she didn't even wait for him to speak.

"Cordell, please, I need your help."

Chapter Ten

"MY MOTHER ALWAYS said an open fire made everything better," Cordell said as he placed another log on the cheerful blaze burning in the stone hearth of the Beargrass Hills living room.

"She would say that having had two boys," Payton said with a weary smile from where she sat on the sofa with a red floral cushion cuddled to her chest. "What is it with fire and boys? I remember a pyromaniac teenage Rhett lighting a campfire every chance he got."

Cordell reclaimed his spot on the sofa. He lifted his arm and Payton again snuggled into his side.

He threaded his fingers into her fragrant hair and massaged her scalp.

"How's the head?"

"Sore. I don't even remembering hitting it, but I've a killer headache."

He slipped his fingers from her hair and brushed aside the silken strands over her forehead to kiss her warm skin.

Silence fell between them, broken only by the pop of an

ember in the fire and the splatter of raindrops on the roof.

"I keep seeing Henry slumped in the truck and Trouble charging," she said in a whisper, tremors wracking her.

"You saved Henry's life." Cordell's arm tightened around her waist. "It mightn't have seemed like it, but you were in control. You moved the truck away from Trouble and somewhere safer and then made sure Henry received help as quickly as possible."

He kept his voice even, pushing back against the surge of his own emotions. He knew firsthand how powerless she'd felt. When he'd answered his cell and heard her desperate words, fear had stripped all warmth from his skin. The time it'd take to grab his bullwhip, saddle Mossy and high tail it to where they were, could mean the difference between finding Payton and Henry safe. Or not.

He locked his jaw to keep both his feelings and thoughts at bay.

"Is he really going to be okay?" she asked, words low and anxious. "He looked so broken lying in the hospital bed."

"He'll be fine. It'll take more than a hit from a bull to keep Henry down. Remember what the doctor said? They've done a CT scan and there's no damage to that hard head of his." He smiled. "I also suspect, from the amount of attention they're paying to his hip, now they have him in hospital they're not letting him go in a hurry."

"Henry does hate hospitals." A small smile curved her lips.

"Is that because he's been in there a lot?"

"No. After his rodeo days ended I think it was thirty years before he set foot inside one again. Anna, his wife, passed away suddenly in her sleep so he didn't spend time in hospitals like I did with Mom."

"You said on the day we met, he hasn't any family? What happened to his sister?"

"Mom said she died when she was in her teens. Anna was an only child and so not only doesn't he have any children but he also has no extended family on her side."

"He has you."

Beneath his arm, Payton stiffened. "Yes and look where that got him. He comes to help and ends up with concussion.'

He hugged her. "It's not your fault."

She didn't answer.

"Rhett looks good for someone who came off second best with Mossy," he said changing the subject.

"He does. Thanks for seeing him and for clearing the air before he left the hospital to go home."

"No problems."

She lifted her head to look at him. "You talked for a long time?"

He kept his expression neutral. Payton didn't need to know their conversation involved where he could find the Taylors. "Did we?"

The ring of the phone in the kitchen saved him from any

further explanation.

"Sit tight," he said, as he stood to answer the phone.

Minutes later, he returned. He stoked the fire to prolong the time until he sat beside Payton.

"Who was it?" she asked as he returned to the sofa and she scooted against his side.

He took a moment to speak. "Henry."

"Good. He must be feeling better if he called."

Cordell nodded, forcing his mind clear of all emotion.

"What did he want?"

"He's up to having visitors."

She leaned away from him to look toward the waning light beyond the living room window. "Now?"

"No, tomorrow, early."

He knew his reply had emerged too terse when her eyes widened.

"Cordell, what's going on?"

"Nothing." He came to his feet. The living room went from being warm and cozy to cold and claustrophobic. "Henry wants company."

She stood too. "I'll grab some blueberry cookies out of the freezer. They'll be thawed for when we visit tomorrow."

Cordell caught her elbow as she turned.

"He only wants one visitor, Pay." He steeled himself. "Me."

Confusion parted her lips. "You?"

"Yes. I can still take him the cookies, if you'd like?"

She pulled her elbow from his grasp and went to sit on the sofa to again hug the cushion. Sadness dulled her eyes.

He sat beside her. "It's okay. It's not that he doesn't want to see you, he … needs to see me."

"What for?"

He scraped a hand around the base of his neck. "He didn't say."

"Would it be because he's mad at me for not calling Brock about the bull like he'd asked me to?"

"No. You're like a daughter to him. He wouldn't be mad or blame you for what happened. He loves you and would be relieved you're okay."

"Then why doesn't he want to see me?"

The deep misery pooling in her gaze moved him far more than if tears had slipped over her cheeks.

He spoke before his emotions could sabotage his thoughts. "I'm certain Henry only wants to see me because somehow he's worked out … the real reason I came to Marietta."

He briefly closed his eyes. It was time to set his secrets free. But for some reason it didn't make what he was about to say any easier. He'd come to heal the wounds of the past but along the way he'd lost his heart as well as his ability to control his feelings.

"Cordell?"

Payton's fingertips brushed his cheek.

He braced himself. Then, he opened his eyes.

"He wants to see me because … I'm his son."

PAYTON STARED AT Cordell's impassive face as though she'd never seen him before. His features may appear as though carved from the same stone as the rugged Montana mountains, but the glitter in his eyes indicated his emotions hovered very close to the surface.

"His son?"

He swallowed and nodded.

"How? He loved Anna, he wouldn't ever have been unfaithful to her?"

"He wasn't." Cordell's voice sounded as rusty as the blades of the windmill she refused to look at. "Ethan and I … happened … before he was married."

The pieces of the jigsaw slotted into place.

"That's why Mossy let Henry lead him without too much fuss. That's why you reminded me of someone. I see now you have Henry's smile." She traced the line of his mouth with a gentle finger. "And you know what, you look a little like the photo Henry has of his father in his office." Her hand lowered. "But then again maybe you don't. Do you have a picture of your mother?"

"I do." He dragged his billfold out of his jeans pocket, flipped open the leather and pulled out a folded photo. She carefully prized it apart. A smiling, dark-haired woman had her arms around two boys.

"She's beautiful." Payton looked closer at the faded color photo. "Perhaps Henry could have known who you were because you have your mother's blue eyes?"

"Maybe, but lots of people have blue eyes. Look at Rhett, he does too and we're in no way related."

She brushed her thumb across the boy on the left, who with his tousled hair and take-no-prisoners stare was obviously Cordell. "You haven't changed."

"I'm not sure that's a good thing. Look at me and what a little hellion I was. Ethan hasn't changed either." Affection softened his tone as he gazed at his brother. "His hair is still always neat and he'd rather talk his way out of trouble."

She handed Cordell the photo. She stayed silent as he replaced the precious photo into his billfold and returned it to his jeans pocket. Outside darkness pressed against the windows but she didn't move to close the drapes. She didn't want to provide any excuse for Cordell to shut down on her. It would be hard for him to embrace his feelings, let alone to talk about a past that would be steeped in painful emotion.

"Where do you want me to start?" he asked as he settled back onto the sofa, strain gouging grooves beside his mouth.

"At the start," she said as she tucked her legs beneath her and faced him.

"It isn't pretty."

She nodded.

An ember in the fire exploded and he stared into the flames. "My mother's father was killed in a tractor accident when she was ten. My grandmother remarried but the younger man she'd thought she knew and she hoped would take care of her and her daughter turned out to be a drunk and a bully. He isolated my grandmother from her family and friends, pulled my mother out of school to be home-schooled and basically kept them prisoner on his remote ranch."

A muscle worked in his jaw at the effort it took to subdue his anger.

"Money was tight so when Rick discovered my mother had a way with horses, he entered her in rodeo events and pocketed the prize money. At the Casper rodeo she didn't do too well and instead of taking his anger out on her in public, he took a whip to her horse."

Payton compressed her lips to contain her own rage.

"Until Henry stopped him."

"That's my Henry."

A smile eased the bleakness in Cordell's eyes.

"Well, a year later, Mom had turned eighteen, she and Henry again met up at the Casper rodeo. By now Mom was allowed to leave the ranch on her own because Rick knew she'd never abandon her mother. Mom and Henry got together but once the weekend ended she went back to the ranch and never saw him again."

"He didn't try to find her?"

"He did. But my mother made sure he couldn't. She gave him a fake number and address. She was under no illusions what Rick would do to Henry if he discovered they'd been together."

"So what happened when she found out she was pregnant?"

"It was a huge shock. But the pregnancy gave her and my grandmother the strength to leave. It took some planning, and all the while they had to hide my mother's pregnancy, but in the end they got away."

"And were you all then safe?"

The fire burned low in the hearth but Payton didn't leave the sofa. Cordell's desolate expression told her more than words could of the fear that had characterized his childhood. "Not for a very long time. But between my mother and grandmother, we were loved and well cared for and somehow they worked enough odd jobs to keep us fed and warm."

"Did he ever find you?"

Cordell's gaze turned gunslinger-cold. "He caught us one winter in South Dakota. In my young imagination we were running from some fire-breathing monster. So when this thin, grey-haired man, reeking of alcohol and stale sweat, grabbed me when I left our trailer I didn't feel afraid. It was only when I saw all the life drain from my mother's eyes I knew this man was the … monster."

The hand Cordell rested on his thigh, fisted. Payton placed her hand over his. His fingers unclenched. He turned his hand until their palms met and he linked his fingers with hers.

"So I bit him," he continued, tone flat, "and punched and kicked him until he let me go. Somehow we all got away."

She swallowed past the emotion in her throat. "Was that the only time he caught up with you?"

"No, he tracked us to Colorado Springs. But by now we were done running. My mother had taken a waitressing job at the local diner and a widowed rancher had started coming in on the days she worked. He then asked her to be his housekeeper and we all moved to his ranch. The following spring they were married."

Payton's eyes misted. "That's so lovely."

"When Rick arrived at the ranch, he didn't stay standing, let alone in our front yard, for long. Scott escorted him to the sheriff's office. About six months later, Mom was on the computer and for the first time ever I saw her cry. But her tears weren't ones of sorrow, just relief. The front page of the local paper of her hometown featured a story about a drunken Rick not making it out of his car wreck alive."

"And you finally were all safe?"

"Yes, we were." Cordell stared at the now flameless fire.

"I'm so glad." She squeezed his hand and stood. "Is Scott still on the Colorado Springs ranch with Ethan?" she asked as she fed two logs onto the fire and used the poker to stir the hot embers.

"No." Sadness threaded Cordell's tone. "One winter we

lost both my grandmother and Scott."

"And your mother?" Payton held her breath as she returned to the sofa.

Eyes hooded, Cordell didn't look away from the now hungry flames. "You might have gained an extra three years with your mother but Ethan and I only got three weeks."

This time the moisture that filled Payton's eyes weren't tears of happiness. "I'm sorry."

She laid her head on his shoulder.

He nodded, still not looking at her. "Six months and three days ago I lost my mother to breast cancer. Six months and five days ago I discovered I had a father called Henry."

Payton lifted her head to look into his drawn face. "You had no idea about Henry?"

"No." Cordell looked away from the fire. "I once asked my mother who my father was and all she said was he was a good man who couldn't be with us. It was only when my mother called Ethan and me to her bedside and handed us a newspaper clipping about Henry winning best all-around cowboy at the Copper Mountain Rodeo, we found out who he really was."

"And Henry never knew about you and Ethan?"

Cordell shook his dark head. "Mom said she didn't tell him at first because it was simply a matter of survival, and then later when she saw a newspaper story about his wedding, she didn't want to ruin his life."

"But now she wanted him to know?"

"She did." He paused, jaw taut. Payton could only imagine how painful his still fresh memories were. "And she said I was the one to do so. But she made me promise I wouldn't waltz in and disrupt his life. I had to make sure it was the right decision to tell him."

"So leasing his land was the perfect chance to get to know him?"

"Yes." A faint smile played across Cordell's lips. "Leasing land closer to Texas for Luke's cattle would have been a whole lot easier. But I still don't know how Henry beat me to it and figured it all out."

"I think I know. You said your mother had a way with horses. That day you stopped the runaway rodeo horse, Henry told me not to be angry with you for taking such a risk because you had a way with horses. I thought he looked shaken because the pram fell over and he'd assumed a baby was inside, but he really looked shaken because he must have known who you really were."

"Maybe. And now he wants to talk to me."

She leaned forward to kiss Cordell and erase the uncertainty from his tense mouth. Tonight's emotions would be nothing compared to talking to the father he'd never known.

"Yes, he does and knowing Henry he'll ask you what took you so long to find him."

She pulled back a little and smiled into Cordell's shadowed eyes. "You have a big day tomorrow and my head is still killing me; I think we both need an early night."

Her smile widened as laughter kindled in his gaze and his face relaxed.

"We do. And with that bad head of yours, I'm going to have to help you out of your clothes all over again."

Chapter Eleven

PAYTON POURED THE last of the water into Mossy's water trough. She sat the empty bucket on the ground and took a second to catch her breath. She really shouldn't carry two buckets at the same time even if it did mean fewer trips. Usually Cordell helped to replenish the horses' water, but it was no surprise he'd headed into Marietta early.

In light of yesterday's drama, it also was no surprise Henry wanted to talk to Cordell. He wouldn't want to waste another day not having things settled between him and his son. She smiled and watched as a magpie landed on the nearby gate. She still couldn't believe Henry was a father. And not to just Cordell, but also to Ethan.

Cordell had briefly left the guest room bed last night to make a call to his brother. He'd then returned with a relieved grin to say Ethan would soon be on the road and would reach Marietta by mid-morning.

Mossy approached and the magpie flew away. The horse hung his head over the fence, and snorted.

She laughed. "Is that your way of saying pretty-please,

Mossy?"

She reached into her jacket pocket. As she usually did when the troughs were full, she fed each horse an apple. Every day Gypsy grew more accustomed to her presence and would shyly extend her nose for a pat. Every day Mossy simply took the apple, glared at Baxter who always stayed close to Payton's legs, and walked away.

Today, Mossy chewed his apple and leaned forward to sniff and then nibble Payton's loose hair. Baxter edged a safe distance away. She touched Mossy's thick neck. When he didn't move, she slid her hand over his velvet-soft coat.

That would be right. She finally won him over and he'd soon be gone. Tension barreled through her and Mossy tossed his head.

"Easy Mossy," she crooned but the moment was lost and he whirled and took off to the far side of his paddock. Gypsy whinnied and followed, galloping along the fence line between them.

Payton looked at Baxter. "You're my witness. Mossy did let me pat him for all of two seconds."

Her light-hearted words didn't fool the kelpie. He whined and wriggled forward to lick her hand. Just like Mossy, the kelpie registered her distress that it wasn't only Mossy who'd soon be gone.

Cordell had been honest from the beginning when he'd said he couldn't stay. A childhood spent moving around had conditioned him to never remain in one spot. He also had a business in Denver to return to. She had no doubt he'd be back; he had a father to get to know and cattle to look after, but he wouldn't be back to be with her. The clock was ticking on her time with him and the day drew nearer when she'd have to pick up the pieces of her life. But it wouldn't be today. Or tomorrow. She took a deep breath and pushed away her sadness.

"It's okay, Baxter Boy. We don't have to say good-bye to Cordell and Mossy just yet." She rubbed behind the kelpie's ears. "Let's go and tackle that muddy pickup. It'll take until lunch to get it clean."

As predicted, cleaning the truck outside, as well as the inside, took an age. She leaned out the open driver's side door to toss a pile of small clods she'd collected from the truck floor when Baxter ran past and barked in the direction of the main gate. She glanced up and saw Cordell's white truck heading their way.

He soon pulled to a stop beside her.

"Having fun?" he asked with a brief grin as he approached. His gaze swept over her as she sat in driver's seat of her truck.

"I'm not sure fun is the right word. Remind me never to get bogged again."

He moved closer to brush his thumb across her jaw. "The truck might be looking clean but you're not."

She leaned forward, expecting him to kiss her. But instead his hand lowered. Cool air replaced the heat of his touch. Eyes fathomless, he moved away to walk around the truck as if to inspect it.

"I think you missed a spot over here."

She slipped from the driver's side seat to follow him. Uncertainty fluttered within her. Something wasn't right. She could only hope his talk with Henry hadn't been a disaster.

She kept her tone light. "Are you volunteering to help? Because I'm getting so much better at letting people help me, you know."

"I do know." He returned her smile but his guarded gaze gave no indication he remembered the ways he'd more than helped her over the past nights. He folded his arms. "But, as much as I'd like to play in the mud, I've come for Mossy."

"Mossy?"

"Yes. I dropped Ethan at Larkspur Ridge to shower and to take a power-nap before we deliver Trouble to his new home. Henry spoke to Brock Sheenan and he's happy to take him on. He also has a quiet bull he wants to talk to you about having in Trouble's place."

"Thanks. Brock has good bulls, I'd definitely be interested in a swap." She examined Cordell's impassive face. "Do you want a quick coffee? I take it all went well with Henry if Ethan is at Larkspur Ridge?"

"Yes, it did. But I'd better not stop for a coffee. I want to ride around the Texan cattle before I collect Ethan." Cordell's arms unfolded. "But you could help me convince Mossy to leave that mustang of yours."

She fell into step beside him and tucked her hand into the back pocket of his Wrangler jeans. His arm looped round her waist. But even with their thighs touching as they walked she couldn't banish the impression a chasm was opening up between them. If all went well with Henry, something else had to be going on?

She assessed his set profile. "So is Henry happy being an instant father?"

"Yes. And you were right. He wanted to know why I took so long to find him, let alone to tell him."

"How did Ethan take him? He can be a little ... gruff."

"Not with Ethan, he isn't. Henry was as sweet as those cookies I left behind on the kitchen bench and he wants you to bring him in this afternoon."

She nodded. "Will do. When you took Ethan to Larkspur Ridge did you notice anything?"

"If you mean the *empty* guest wing Rosa always keeps ready, yes, I did."

"I told you he was a rogue when you turned up for cookies and a place to stay." She toyed with a button on his shirt. "I'm glad he didn't offer you bed."

An unexpected bleakness washed across his blue gaze before his mouth lowered to hers.

His kiss ended all too soon.

"At this rate," he said, breaking eye contact and taking a step away, "I won't get Mossy caught let alone saddled. So Miss Muddy Cowgirl, I'll take it from here, and let you get back to cleaning that pickup of yours."

PAYTON RETURNED CORDELL'S wave as he drove his truck and trailer past her on his way out. Uneasiness settled into the pit of her stomach. She wiped the last smear of mud from the truck door and dropped the rag into the sudsy bucket of water at her feet. She couldn't shake the feeling Cordell wasn't just driving out of Beargrass Hills, he was also driving out of her life.

She watched until she could no longer see the back of the trailer, then busied herself putting away the hose and the buckets. But the more she occupied her hands, the more her thoughts raced. As much as she didn't want to admit it, instinct and the emotional distance she'd just sensed between them, told her their time together had expired. Cordell had fulfilled his promise to his mother and now was getting ready to leave.

Throat aching, she looked at Baxter. "You're in charge, Baxter Boy. I can't stand around here moping, I'm taking a road trip to deliver Henry his cookies."

She'd relinquished control and allowed Cordell into her world. It was her own fault she'd now have her heart broken. He hadn't expressed himself with words but the tenderness of his touch let her know she was more than a casual fling. She wasn't just another risk he'd taken to challenge himself that he couldn't feel.

She turned for a last look at the undulating foothills where Cordell would now be checking the Texan cattle. The scenery blurred into a swathe of green.

But Rhett hadn't been right. She wasn't Cordell's girl. And he wasn't her cowboy. Her heart bled. No matter how much she wanted him to be.

CORDELL LIFTED HIS right hand from the steering wheel and flexed his bruised knuckles.

He shot Ethan a quick look. "When we see Payton, we don't need to go into too much detail about where we just were."

The smile Ethan flashed him in the dim light of the truck cabin could have been his own. "I can't wait to meet the cowgirl who has tamed my big bad brother."

"When you do, remember I'm supposed to be taking fewer risks and living less dangerously. And tackling the Taylors doesn't exactly fall into those two categories."

Ethan chuckled. "Tell Payton the truth, you talked first and they listened. Which they did until the older Taylor decided he was done with your jabbering."

"What was wrong with my jabbering? You were the one who told me to not go in with all guns blazing."

"I did but next time you talk your way out of trouble, at least try and look a little friendlier. That death-glare of yours would snap-freeze a lake."

"Next time, you can do the talking and I'll be the back-up."

Ethan flexed his own bruised hand. "After our 'conversation' there won't be a next time. I've no doubt the Taylors are on their way to Reno like they said they would be."

"It was thanks to Payton's cowboy friend, Rhett, we found them. He had no idea they were into anything illegal until the night they stole Mossy for him to ride. The youngest brother let slip their trailer hadn't only ever carried a stolen horse."

"Well, their thieving days are over. The relief on their widowed aunt's face was worth taking all three of them on. The sheriff will visit in the morning to sort out who owns the cattle we found corralled for re-branding. He said he'd make a few calls so when the Taylors reach Reno they'll have some charges to face."

Cordell lowered his headlights as a car passed. They'd soon be at Larkspur Ridge where he'd leave Ethan for the night. He glanced at his brother who smothered a yawn.

"Thanks for your help today. I know how tired you are after driving all night."

He rolled his shoulders against his own weariness. He hadn't slept well. Not because he was worried about his morning talk with Henry but because every time he closed his eyes he saw Payton being crushed by Trouble.

"It's been a day I won't forget in a hurry," Ethan replied. "Meeting Henry. Taking that bad-tempered bull to Brock's.

And talking to the Taylors. I haven't had this much fun since you moved to Denver and life become dull and boring."

Cordell laughed but when Ethan glanced at him, he knew his twin had sensed the strain beneath his amusement.

"You okay with how things have worked out?" Ethan asked.

He nodded. "Henry is a tough but a good man. Even without knowing about us, he spent years looking for Mom. He'd realized she hadn't been in a safe place. He was glad to hear she'd found happiness with Scott and that he'd loved us and raised us as if we were his own."

In front of them the ranch house lights twinkled in the darkness from the top of an invisible hill.

"So are you staying?" Ethan asked, voice quiet.

He didn't even try to misunderstand what Ethan had asked. He took his time to speak. "One minute, I am. And the next, I'm not so sure. She could do so much better than me."

"According to Henry, she doesn't want anyone but you."

"I have no idea how Henry knows such a thing."

"Maybe he just knows Payton?"

He grunted. "Maybe."

Ethan laughed softy. "You are so Henry's son. You're even grunting like him now."

But Cordell didn't join in with his brother's mirth. His heart felt like it was about to rip in two.

BAXTER BARKED FROM within the warmth of his kennel nestled beneath the pine tree as Cordell parked his truck beside the barn. He made no effort to move. Payton had left the porch light on and its soft pool of light beckoned him inside. Still he didn't leave the truck. His bruised hand tightened around the steering wheel until his breath hissed.

Physical pain was nothing compared to his internal torment. All his life he'd blanked out his emotions and now they appeared hell bent on revenge. Twisting and bucking, they gave him no peace or respite. Payton said his emotions made him human but all they did was cause him anguish. They rendered him vulnerable and they made him feel inadequacy and fear.

He'd been lucky Mossy had his wits about him when they'd driven Trouble away from Payton and Henry because he sure didn't have his. When they'd arrived to find Payton outside the truck, branch in hand waiting for the bull to charge, he hadn't been able to breathe, let alone focus.

What would happen if Trouble got past Mossy? What would happen if he failed to protect Payton? What would happen if he lost the woman he loved?

And ever since his fear hadn't left him.

He sighed and he released his clamped grip on the steering wheel. His heart told him to stay, he did deserve a special woman like Payton. But his mind told him the only way to remain safe and to not feel was to keep moving.

He made his way inside. In the kitchen he saw a foil-covered plate on the bench. His chest tightened. Payton had kept dinner for him. The living room fire crackled and he headed into the warm room. She lay asleep on the sofa, feet bare and a handmade red floral quilt covering her.

Breathing ragged, he bent to caress her smooth cheek.

The only place he'd ever want to be was by his beautiful and brave cowgirl's side.

She murmured his name and he bent to kiss her. She twined her hands around his neck and kissed him. A slow, sweet kiss that he never wanted to end.

He could do this. He could silence the demons inside. He could learn to live with his emotions, no matter how defenseless they made him.

He gathered Payton in his arms and she snuggled into his neck. He filled his lungs with her floral scent. He could never look at a perfumed beargrass wildflower again without thinking of her.

He carried her along the hallway heading for his bed, but as he drew near to her bedroom door. He stopped.

He'd ridden badass bulls. He'd braved Mossy's wrath. He could do this. He could take the ultimate risk and tell her he loved her. He could stay. He took a step toward his own room. Blood pounded in his ears. Fear choked him. He again stopped.

Legs leaden, he turned to walk through Payton's doorway. He gently laid her on the bed and pulled the covers to her chin. Head bowed, he quit the room, without once looking back.

Chapter Twelve

PAYTON AWOKE TO two thoughts. She was in her own bed. Alone. And that she wasn't going to lose Cordell. She mightn't have any control over him leaving but that didn't mean she couldn't fight for her cowboy. She needed to tell him how she felt and then she needed to ask him to stay.

She scrambled out of bed. She still wore her clean jeans and pink western shirt she'd put on to visit Henry after lunch yesterday. Trinity would cringe at her wardrobe selection but the creased and unromantic outfit would have to do. It wasn't what she wore that was important, just the three simple words she had to say.

But when she saw Cordell's door open, the bed made and a packed duffle on the floor, her stomach plummeted to her bare toes. She drew a calming breath. Maria and Joe were returning that night, Cordell was simply getting ready to move into the bunkhouse.

But as she sped along the hallway to see if he was in the kitchen, the tremble in her hands said she didn't believe such an explanation. She pushed open the kitchen door but the room was also empty save for a small note on the table. The line of her rigid shoulders relaxed as she scanned Cordell's message. He wasn't leaving.

He'd left early to collect Ethan to have breakfast with Henry. He'd then spend the morning showing Ethan around Marietta and would bring Henry home to Larkspur Ridge after lunch. He'd see her then.

She bit the inside of her cheek. She now had over half a day until she would have a chance to talk to him. She needed a plan and failing that she needed to bake cookies. She reached for her cell phone that sat next to the microwave oven. Instinct cautioned her she'd only have one chance to convince Cordell to stay. Now there wasn't such a rush to speak to him, her jeans and western shirt had to go. She needed all the ammunition she could get. What she really needed was a makeover.

She dialed Mandy's number.

"Hi, Payton," Mandy answered.

"Hi, Mandy. Is today still your day off?"

"Yes, it's Monday. Why?"

"Are you sitting down?"

"No, but I am now."

"Good. Can you please style my hair?"

Payton held the phone away from her ear as Mandy squealed. "You bet. Cut and blow-dry?"

"Anything."

"Anything?" Mandy's voice grew incredulous. "Who are you and where is the real Beargrass Hills cowgirl called Payton Hollis?"

She chuckled. "Anything goes as long as I don't have a pixie cut. Do you remember we all got them in high school? My neck has never felt so cold."

Mandy laughed. "Now there's my practical girl."

"Are you still sitting?"

"Yes."

"I also need to … shop for a … dress."

Silence. Then, "Pay, is everything okay?" Seriousness wiped all amusement from Mandy's words.

"It will be."

"You know Cordell will love you just the way you are?"

A lump formed in her throat at her friend's concern. "I'm hoping so. I don't want to change who I am, I just need some sort of … secret weapon."

"Secret weapons are good, especially if they come with sky-high stilettos. I always said you'd change your mind about wearing heels."

"No heels."

"Okay then, we'll pin that one for later. You know Trinity will hate to miss all the action. She has had a client cancel, the little girl has chicken pox, so she might have some time. I'll text her. I think we're going to need sugar, and it's a nice day outside, so how about I meet you at the ice cream store and we formulate our game plan? Text me when you leave."

"Will do. And Mandy, thanks."

"You're welcome." She laughed. "And don't think you've gotten out of giving me a proper explanation for all of this."

"Not for a minute. Is now a good time to change the subject and say Cordell's twin brother is in town?"

Again she held the phone away from her ear as Mandy squealed. "Do hurry up, Payton, we have so much to talk about."

BUT AS PAYTON sat in Crawford Park outside the domed courthouse playing with her uneaten vanilla ice cream she thankfully couldn't get a word in. While Mandy and Trinity debated the color of her soon-to-be inflicted foils, she watched the golden autumn leaves drift to the ground from the park's flame-bright trees. Normally the sight filled her with a sense of peace, but not today. Until she convinced Cordell to stay, a hard ball of concern was permanently lodged in her midriff.

Trinity checked her watch and pushed her cookies n' cream ice cream over to Payton. She usually finished Trinity's leftovers and to Mandy and Trinity's disgust she then never had trouble fitting into her jeans. But this time she couldn't even finish her own serving.

"Yes, okay," Trinity said as she stood, "go with caramel highlights but only subtle ones." She pulled her fitted jacket over the waist of her charcoal-grey pencil skirt. "I've got to run. My next appointment is in fifteen minutes. But I'll be right to come shopping for a dress in my lunch break."

"Good luck," she said as she hugged Payton, whispering in her ear, "*subtle* caramel highlights, okay?"

Payton waved as Trinity then headed toward her speech pathologist office across town at the east end of Bramble Lane in time for her next small client.

Mandy picked up her mocha toffee ice cream and as she ate her gaze remained fixed on Payton's unruly, over-long hair.

Payton shifted on the park bench. "No pixie cut, remember?"

Mandy's gleeful smile failed to offer any reassurance. "But otherwise anything else is fine?"

She sighed. "Do your worst."

WHAT FELT LIKE a lifetime later, Payton prized herself out of the hair salon chair and dutifully followed Mandy over to where Trinity sat flicking through a thick magazine. Trinity sprang to her feet, her smile wide.

"Look at you, Pay. Cordell doesn't stand a chance." She touched the glossy, loose curls that fell onto Payton's right shoulder. "Mandy, you are genius."

Mandy gave a small bow. "Thank you." She smoothed away a lock of hair that had fallen onto Payton's forehead. "It does help having such a beautiful blank canvas to work with."

Heat filled Payton's cheeks. "Thanks but this is all your work, Mandy. Come tomorrow and you'll be seeing the real Payton again."

Mandy winked. "After what I've done to your hair I guarantee we won't be seeing you or Cordell for days."

She chewed on her lip. She could only hope so.

Mandy frowned. "Payton ..."

Payton released her lip. "Sorry. I know you told me not to do that. I'll ruin my lipstick."

Trinity grinned. "Nice make-up job, too, Mandy. Not too heavy but just enough. I never knew your eyes were so golden, Pay, or your lashes so long."

"That's because," Mandy said, "she has a record for applying *all* her make-up in under five minutes and she doesn't ever blend."

Trinity's brows lifted. "What are we going to do with you, Pay?"

Payton linked arms with her best friends. "Take me shopping."

Trinity laughed. "Yes, that will do as we know how much you hate trying on clothes."

As they left the hair salon, Payton stopped and looked left along Main Street toward the Java Café. "Trinity, hadn't we better get you something to eat before we shop? This is your lunch break."

"No, I'm right. I grabbed some yoghurt and fruit from

the fridge at work before I left. Do you and Mandy want anything?"

They both shook their heads.

"I'm still full from the ice cream," Mandy said, "that will teach me to get a large serving."

"So am I," Payton lied, gazing past the café to where she could make out the sign for Marietta Western Wear in the next block.

"Don't even think about it," Trinity scolded. "We're shopping for a dress not for jeans and western shirts."

"This way," Mandy said pulling Payton along to the boutique one store down from the hair salon.

She walked through the doorway. A bell tingled, announcing their arrival. An elegant sales associate smiled as she looked up from the paperwork she was completing on the counter. The boutique smelt of jasmine and the soft music piped around the brightly lit store completed the impression of luxurious extravagance.

Payton hesitated. What was she doing? She shouldn't be splurging money on a dress? She still had her favorite boots to fix.

Trinity gave her a little push from behind. "Pay, it's my treat. You never let me buy anything for your birthday or Christmas and you are always baking me cookies or bringing me vegetables."

The sales clerk shuffled her paperwork together and beamed at them. "Anything I can help you with, ladies?"

Mandy stepped forward. "Yes, please. We need a dress. And not just any dress. One that will make a cowboy's jaw drop."

"Pay," Trinity said softly from beside her, "it really is okay. Mandy has done your hair and make-up. Please let me do this for you."

"You really don't have to."

"I know. I want to."

"Thank you"

Trinity hugged her. "That's what friends are for. Now let's get shopping."

Payton's head spun after the first two dresses were held up against her. After five, the colors and expensive fabrics all merged into a rainbow of chaos.

"Too short. Too dowdy. Too sexy. Not sexy enough."

Mandy and Trinity's words swirled around her in an ever-increasing crescendo of sound.

She sank into the chair that would usually be reserved for long-suffering males lured into the boutique by a woman's smile and bedroom promises. She was never going shopping again.

Then she spied a white dress. Against the sea of color and movement it spoke of peace and simplicity. She came to her feet and collected the dress from the rack. Falling to above the knee with a nipped-in waist, the skirt featured a white lace overlay. She hesitated and then returned the dress to the rack. The bodice was far too plunging.

Trinity whisked it off the rack. "Don't you dare put this back. This is perfect."

Payton stopped herself from chewing on her lip. She recognized the resolute note in Trinity's voice. When Trinity put her mind to something she usually got her way.

"Trin, wearing your pink strapless dress to Eliza's wedding just about killed me. It felt like it would slip off whenever I breathed. Who knows what Cordell got an eyeful of when I helped him with the calf? I just wouldn't be comfortable wearing a dress that shows more than it hides."

Mandy nodded. "Even though I'm sure red-blooded Cordell wouldn't mind an eyeful, let alone, the low bodice, I agree, it's not who you are, Payton. But I do have a solution." She went to a shelf and unfolded a white lace camisole. "You'd have something like this at home that you could wear underneath. It would have to have a touch of lace on it though to match the dress."

"Sorry, there's no camisole, let alone any lace, in my closet."

Mandy groaned. "No lace at all?"

"Nope."

"Poor Cordell. Next shopping trip we are not going to buy a dress."

Trinity held the white dress against Payton. "Try it on."

Payton glanced at the sales clerk who'd returned to her paperwork after it'd become obvious Payton had two enthusiastic fashion gurus helping her.

She smiled. "Do try it on. Your friends are right, the lace camisole underneath will work really well."

Payton touched the soft lace of the overskirt. "The dress would look good with boots."

"No," both Trinity and Mandy chorused.

"Yes. I'm sorry, Mandy, I'm not coming over to the dark side and wearing heels. Besides Cordell says his fantasy is boots not heels, anyway."

Trinity's and Mandy's eyes grew round.

"Tell us more," said Mandy, her voice slightly breathless.

Payton chuckled. "And spoil the fun of your fertile imaginations? I don't think so. But, I will try on the dress."

When she emerged long minutes later, she knew she'd found the right outfit. With the fitted camisole underneath, the plunging neckline wasn't an issue. The dress was perfect. The fine weave of the fabric caressed her legs and she did a little twirl.

Tears glistened in Mandy's eyes. "Cordell won't be able to leave."

Trinity nodded, her smile wistful. "It's a wrap. That's the one."

Payton hugged Trinity and then Mandy. "I expect to repay the secret weapon favor for each of you when the time is right."

"It's a deal." Mandy hugged her back. "Now go get your cowboy, Pay."

Chapter Thirteen

THE BUTTERFLIES MAKING their home in her middle threatened to take flight as Payton saw Cordell's pickup beside the barn.

Just. Breathe.

She parked her own truck in its usual position adjacent to the corral. Smoothing her hair like Mandy had showed her, she slicked her lips in the sweet-tasting pink gloss Mandy had slipped into her bag.

She swallowed and opened the door. Her secret weapon had to work. If her plan failed, the days of knowing Cordell waited inside the ranch house for her, were numbered.

But as she left her truck, she turned right instead of heading toward the front porch. From over near the horses she'd caught a flash of red plaid and denim. She walked around the barn and for the first time in what felt like a lifetime, she looked at the windmill. She kept her chin high to stop her tears falling.

Not a day passed when she didn't miss the infectious chuckle of her father's laughter and the warmth of her mother's gentle smile. But Cordell was right. Letting go of the control she clung to both empowered and made her stronger. Knowing that he would soon be there to help with an unconscious Henry had given her the extra strength she'd needed to hold off Trouble until Cordell and Mossy arrived. Just like her pioneering forebears, she didn't have to fight every battle on her own. It wasn't a sign of weakness to ask for, and accept, help.

Her steps slowed. From the back, the cowboy talking to Mossy looked familiar but something was off. The man gazed across the valley and she glimpsed a profile that wasn't Cordell's.

Ethan.

She must have spoken his name because he swung around. His tanned face broke into a smile that resembled both Cordell's and Henry's.

She walked forward. "Hi, you must be Ethan."

Ethan took off his hat and extended a hand. "And you must be Payton?"

"Yes, I am." She returned his handshake. "Welcome to Montana."

"Thanks."

Up close she could see subtle differences between the twin brothers. Ethan's eyes might be the same clear blue, but whereas Cordell's were as turbulent as a storm-fed creek, his were as calm and as steady as a still pond. The strong line of his jaw hinted at a strength equal to Cordell's, but a strength that would be quiet and considered.

Realizing she was staring, she quickly slipped her fingers from his.

The breeze teased her hair and fine windblown strands clung to the gloss on her lips. She brushed them away with a quick hand. So much for making a good first impression on the brother of the man she loved. She was wearing makeup and a dress and looked nothing like a working cowgirl who wanted to be taken seriously.

"Your mustang mare is a little beauty," Ethan said with a wide smile. And in his smile she saw all the lightness and laughter Cordell had gifted to his brother by shouldering the darkness of their childhood.

"She is. I was hoping she'd teach bossy Mossy some manners."

Ethan chuckled. "I'm afraid it's too late for that."

Mossy bared his teeth and leaned over the fence to swipe at Ethan's arm. Ethan casually moved away.

"Mossy, that wasn't very nice," Payton said with a frown.

"It's okay, it's not personal," Ethan said, taking a step closer to the fence. As Mossy again bared his teeth, Ethan reached out to rub the horse's neck. To her surprise Mossy's ears flickered forward and he lowered his head.

"I don't blame him for being ornery. He associates seeing me with Cordell leaving as I'm the one who then looks after him."

A chill replaced the warmth of the autumn sun on her

bare arms.

She took a second to speak. "And this time?"

"The same deal," Ethan said not meeting her eyes.

All sound faded. All sensation ebbed. All she could hear was the desperate pounding of her heart. She'd left it too late to fight for her cowboy. Cordell's duffle hadn't been packed to move into the bunkhouse.

"When?" she managed.

"This afternoon. He used my sedan to bring Henry home as it would be more comfortable than his truck. So after he's checked his cattle, he'll swap vehicles, load his gear and then I imagine he'll hit the road. Knowing him he'll want to get into the office early tomorrow."

"What about Mossy and the Texan cattle?"

"I'm staying for a couple of weeks to spend time with Henry, so I'll check the cattle and also feed Mossy while I'm here. I'll talk to Cordell, and then when I go I might take Mossy and the trailer home with me to Colorado Springs."

She barely nodded. Her life was unraveling way too fast. Just like that, Cordell would be gone. And from Ethan's solemn tone she had no doubt when he did return it wouldn't be for long. He'd see Henry, check the cattle and then be off again. She squared her shoulders. She wasn't done fighting. Until Cordell drove his truck through the main gate she wasn't giving up stopping him from leaving.

Ethan rubbed his jaw. "I heard the sedan pull up, if you want to go and catch him before he swaps vehicles."

"Thanks." She angled her chin. "I do."

Payton strode from the horse paddocks to the barn in record time. Cordell had parked Ethan's conservative white sedan beside his truck. Back to her, he lowered the tailgate of his pickup. The driver's side door was already open as if he needed a fast get-away. She slowed her breathing and strove for calm. This couldn't be the last time she saw his Wrangler clad-butt and the snug stretch of his western shirt across his broad shoulders.

She knew the moment he realized she approached. He stiffened and slowly turned.

Her hair and dress had the desired effect.

His jaw didn't drop. His face was a carved and immobile mask. But everything she needed and hoped to see was in his eyes. Hunger, longing, pain all flashed across his gaze in quick succession before a shutter descended over his emotions. The hope within her wavered. Her secret weapon hadn't succeeded.

"So when were you going to tell me?" Her question emerged far more shaky than strong.

"Tell you what?" Wariness slowed his words as he glanced at the knuckles on his right hand.

"That you were leaving for good."

He frowned even as his mouth tensed. "My brother tell you that?"

"He did." She looked toward where Ethan still remained near the horses.

Cordell crossed his arms as his stare travelled slowly from the top of her blow-dried head to the tips of her scuffed boots. When he'd finished his thorough examination, her breaths were shallow and her hormones were over-heating. Her body might have only one thing on its to-do list but her mind had a plan to follow.

"You look … incredible," he said, words husky. His darkened gaze returned to the tight white lace of the camisole that filled the gap left by the dress's plunging neckline.

"Don't try and change the subject."

He sighed. "I'm not. Here …" He unfolded his arms and turned to reach into the pickup tray. He pulled out her favorite broken boots and the ripped horse rug she'd wrapped the abandoned calf in. "I'll give you these before I get too … distracted. They've all been fixed."

"Thanks."

Never had a word been so hard to say. It was as though even speaking posed a threat to the tight grip she held on her tenuous self-control. Cordell might be leaving and yet he still looked out for her. He'd known the boots and the rug had needed mending without her saying anything and had taken them to Marietta to be repaired. He felt something for her even if he wasn't prepared to act upon it and stay. It was all the encouragement she needed to change his mind.

"Payton —"

She closed the distance between them and pressed a finger to his lips. "I need to say something first," she said in a firm voice, "and I hope it will change your mind about leaving. If it doesn't then I hope one day you'll find somewhere you feel safe enough to never leave." She paused and fought to speak past the emotions stealing her composure. "I love –"

The rest of her words were lost in a gasp as Cordell's warm hands secured her waist and he lifted her onto the tailgate. Even before her butt landed on the cold metal, his urgent mouth claimed hers. He kissed her like a man who had found a place to call home. A man who wasn't ever going to leave.

She locked her arms around his neck to let him know she was never letting him go. Even if this was their good-bye kiss.

The clearing of a throat broke them apart. Chest heaving, she looked across to where Ethan rested his hip against his sedan. She saw the brothers exchange a long and serious look before Cordell rasped, "You say too much."

Ethan grinned and winked. "You can thank me later."

Cordell rested his forehead on hers and they remained silent, letting their ragged breaths do the talking, while Ethan reversed and drove away.

Still uncertain, despite their kiss and the possessive way he held her, of where the conversation was heading, she remained silent.

"You don't know it," Cordell said, drawing back a little and touching her cheekbone. Against her skin she could feel the shake in his fingers. "But my non-risk taking brother just lived dangerously. Did he say anything else when he told you I was leaving?"

Her hands slid from around his neck to grip his shoulders. "He said he might take Mossy home with him."

Cordell chuckled. "And you think Henry is a rogue. Mossy isn't going anywhere. And neither am I. What Ethan didn't say was that I'd be back in a week ... for good."

"For good?" she said, a catch in her voice.

"Yes." Emotion fired in his eyes, emotion he didn't try and repress. "I've found somewhere I feel safe." His lips touched her temple. "And that's wherever you are."

"Are you sure?"

She wasn't even certain she'd asked the question, let alone that it had been coherent and audible.

"I had to think my way through it, but I've never been surer of anything in my life. Just like I've never been as scared as when I had to protect you from Trouble. I didn't think I could deal with the fear of anything happening to you but the alternative is to not be with the woman that I ... love." He pulled her even closer. "And that isn't an option." The white flash of his smile brought tears to her eyes. "I love you too, Pay."

The tenderness of his slow and thorough kiss silenced the last of her inner doubts that being by her side was where her cowboy wanted to stay.

"A week will be an eternity," she said as they drew apart.

"I know, but it will give me time to complete the sale of my consultancy business to my manager and to pack up my condo." Happiness intensified the blue of his eyes as he glanced toward the rugged mountain backdrop behind her. "I can't say I'll be sad to leave Denver."

He tangled his fingers through her hair and lowered his mouth to speak against her lips. "Once Luke's cattle have returned to Texas I'll buy some of my own. Then there could be a few things for a cowboy to do around here if a certain stubborn cowgirl will let him help out."

She nodded, incapable of words. It had rained and now Beargrass Hills would also have a team at the helm, just like in the days when her parents had run the ranch. The responsibility of preserving her home wouldn't rest solely on her shoulders. She lifted her mouth to his, accepting all the help he'd ever offer.

When their kiss ended, Cordell took a step back. "I've got something else for you."

She reluctantly let him go. He moved to the driver's side seat, leaned in and pulled out a bunch of pink roses.

Her heart swelled. They were from the old pioneer rose bush at the cabin that she'd always picked blooms from with her mother.

He handed them to her with a gravity that promised her a lifetime of love and flowers.

"Luckily, I took these out of the sedan before that meddling brother of mine left. Little did he know, I wasn't going to leave without telling you how I felt and that I'd be back to stay."

She breathed in the faint perfume of the delicate pink buds and then placed the roses onto the tailgate beside her. She clasped the front of Cordell's shirt to pull him against her.

"Just as well, cowboy, because on page one of the sassy and modern cowgirls' manual it says to never let go of your man."

He smiled a crooked grin. "I hope there's also something in there about how to say goodbye to your cowboy who you won't be seeing for a long and lonely week?"

"There could be." She hooked her legs around him, her fingers skimming the hot, smooth skin where his shirt opened. He shuddered beneath her caress. "Help me get out of this dress and you'll find out."

"I thought you'd never ask." His mouth found the sweet spot at the base of her throat before he lifted her from the tailgate and held her tight. "But the lace and the boots stay on."

The End

If you enjoyed **Cherish Me, Cowboy**, you'll love the other Big Sky Maverick stories!

Wildflower Ranch Series

Book 1: Cherish Me, Cowboy

Book 2: Her Mistletoe Cowboy

Book 3: Her Big Sky Cowboy

Book 4: His Outback Cowgirl

Available now at your favorite online retailer!

ABOUT THE AUTHOR

When not writing **Alissa Callen** plays traffic controller to four children, three dogs, two horses and one renegade cow who really does believe the grass is greener on the other side of the fence. After a childhood spent chasing sheep on the family farm, she has always been drawn to remote areas and small towns, even when residing overseas. Once a teacher and a counsellor, she remains interested in the life journeys people take. Her books are characteristically heart-warming, emotional and character driven. She currently lives on a small slice of rural Australia.

Thank you for reading

CHERISH ME, COWBOY

If you enjoyed this book, you can find more from all our great authors at TulePublishing.com, or from your favorite online retailer.

Made in the USA
Las Vegas, NV
15 September 2024